Home to Lost Creek

Riverbend Valley Book #7

Tara Baisden

Sterling Ridge Press LLC

Copyright

Cover designed by Sterling Ridge Press LLC

Published by: Sterling Ridge Press, LLC www.sterlingridgepress.com

ISBN: 978-1-966093-29-9 Printed in the United States of America

First Edition: July 2025

For permissions, contact: tara@tarabaisden.com or visit www.tarabaisden.com

Dedication

For every heart that's weathered a storm and dared to dream again.
For the faithful who whisper Bible verses into the darkness, trusting
that light will eventually break through.
For single parents who carry worlds on their shoulders while making
sure little ones never feel the weight.
For those who've returned to hometowns and found not what was left
behind, but what was waiting to be discovered.
And especially for you, dear reader, who knows that sometimes the
most beautiful love stories aren't about finding someone new but
recognizing someone who's been there all along.
May you always find your way back home.
With gratitude and love,
Tara

About Riverbend Valley

Welcome to the fictional town of Riverbend Valley, Montana!

Nestled in the shadow of the breathtaking Sapphire Mountains, Riverbend Valley is a place where life flows as peacefully as the rivers winding through it. Surrounded by rolling ranch lands, dense forests, and the rugged peaks of Montana's wilderness, this picturesque valley is the perfect setting for tales of faith, love, and second chances.

<u>A Rugged Heritage</u>

Founded in the late 1800s by homesteaders drawn to the fertile land and expansive views, Riverbend Valley began as a ranching settlement. Riverbend Valley's roots run deep, forged by generations of ranchers and cowboys who've worked the land with grit and determination. This is a place where faith has always been a cornerstone, guiding its people through hardships and celebrating their triumphs. From the well-worn pews of Riverbend Valley Community Church to the lively gatherings at the rodeo grounds, Riverbend Valley's traditions reflect a steadfast commitment to God, family, and the land.

<u>A Community of Faith</u>

Riverbend Valley offers a refuge for weary souls and a chance to rediscover the beauty of life's simple pleasures. Whether it's through a quiet moment of prayer along the river, a moonlit ride under Montana skies, or the laughter of a community united in celebration, this is a place where hearts are mended, faith is renewed, and love abounds.

<u>The Essence of Small-Town Life</u>

With a population of just over three thousand, Riverbend Valley retains its small-town charm. Main Street is lined with family-owned businesses, from the Bluebird Café, famous for its huckleberry pies, to the General Mercantile, where locals gather to swap stories and stock up on supplies. Seasonal festivals bring the community together, from the Spring Rodeo to the Fall Harvest Festival, celebrating the rhythms of life in this ranching town.

<u>A Haven for Visitors</u>

Visitors to Riverbend Valley are captivated by its rustic charm and natural beauty. Whether it's horseback riding through the foothills, fishing in the Deer Run River, or stargazing from Silver Bluff's iconic overlook, there's something for everyone to enjoy.

Experience the Heart of Riverbend Valley

Here, under the endless skies and among the resilient people of Montana, you'll find stories of redemption, second chances, and unwavering faith. Riverbend Valley isn't just a setting—it's a celebration of the rugged heritage and timeless grace that make this place unforgettable.

Welcome to Riverbend Valley, where faith is strong, family is everything, and love always finds a way.

I hope you fall in love with its enduring spirit.

Contents

Chapter 1

The fence post fought him with the stubborn determination of something that had weathered forty Montana winters, but Cade Mayer wasn't about to let a piece of rotted timber win. Sweat traced a path down his spine beneath his denim work shirt as he leveraged the post puller against the embedded wood, muscles straining until the post finally surrendered with a satisfying crack.

He'd been working this particular stretch of fence line for the past hour, replacing posts and stretching new wire with precision. Physical labor suited him; it kept his hands busy and his mind mercifully quiet. The repetitive motions of ranch work provided a rhythm that drowned out thoughts he preferred not to entertain, thoughts that had a way of creeping in during idle moments like wolves circling a campfire.

The new post slid into the hole with satisfying ease. Cade packed dirt around its base with firm, economical movements, testing its stability with a practiced shake before moving to thread the barbed wire through the metal clips. This section of pasture bordered the main barn complex on Lost Creek Ranch, close enough to hear the gentle lowing of cattle in the holding pens and the occasional whinny from the horses in the nearby paddock. The sounds of ranch life had become his sanctuary—honest, predictable, and demanding nothing from him except competence and reliability.

A meadowlark called from somewhere in the nearby pasture, its liquid notes floating across the grassland where Black Angus cattle grazed in contentment. The familiar sight should have brought him satisfaction—it was good land, well-managed, the kind of operation his father and grandfather would have admired. Instead, it served as a constant reminder of what he'd lost, what had been taken from him by a woman who'd promised to love him through better and worse but had chosen better elsewhere.

The sound of of someone approaching pulled him from his brooding. Cade straightened, wiping his hands on his jeans as Chuck Turner and his wife, Ruby, walked his way. At fifty-six, Chuck carried himself with the easy confidence of a man who'd spent his life working land that his family had owned for three generations. His graying hair barely showed beneath his well-worn Stetson, and his weathered face spoke of countless hours under the Montana sun. Ruby, two years younger but with the same salt-of-the-earth bearing, moved with the brisk efficiency of a woman who'd raised a daughter and held her family together, while teaching elementary school and helping run a ranch.

"Afternoon, Cade," Chuck called out, his voice carrying the warm respect that had characterized their working relationship from the beginning. "Making good progress on that fence line."

"Should have it finished soon," Cade replied. In the eight months since Chuck had hired him as foreman, they'd developed an easy rapport built on mutual respect and shared understanding of ranch life.

Chuck never micromanaged, trusting Cade's expertise, while Cade appreciated the older man's steady leadership and fair treatment. It wasn't the same as owning his own spread, but it was honest work with good people, more than many men could claim.

Ruby stepped forward with a warm smile. "You work too hard, Cade. When's the last time you took some time off?"

"Can't say as I remember," he admitted, which was the truth. Since Rachel had walked out and the divorce had cost him everything, work had become both his salvation and his penance. Idle hours led to dwelling on failure, and dwelling on failure led to the kind of dark thoughts that had no place in a man's mind.

"Well, that's going to have to change," Ruby said with gentle authority. "We've got some exciting news to share. Our Eva's moving home tomorrow."

The name hit him like a physical blow, stealing the breath from his lungs and making his hands unconsciously clench at his sides. Eva. After twelve years, she was coming back to Riverbend Valley. Images flashed through his mind—brown hair catching sunlight as she laughed at something he'd said, blue eyes sparkling with mischief as she challenged him to race their horses to the creek, and the soft warmth of her hand in his as they walked along this very fence line during their senior year of high school.

"Eva," he repeated, his voice sounding strange and distant to his ears. "I didn't know she was..." He stopped, clearing his throat and trying to regain his composure. "That's good. Really good. You must be excited to have her close again."

Chuck and Ruby exchanged a look that spoke of decades of marriage and silent communication. Chuck nodded slowly, studying Cade's reaction with the perceptive eyes of a man who'd seen enough of life to recognize emotional storms when they gathered.

"She's been teaching in Bozeman since college," Ruby explained, her tone carefully neutral. "I'm not sure if you knew she inherited Connie's old place when she passed two years ago. The bed and breakfast has just been sitting empty while Eva tried to decide what to do with it. She finally made up her mind to give small-town life a try again."

"She's got a son," Chuck added. "Noah. He's eight now. Good boy. Lost his daddy before he was even born."

The words hit Cade with unexpected force. Eva was a widow. The knowledge shouldn't have mattered—shouldn't have created the strange tightness in his chest or the unwelcome surge of protective instinct that he'd thought he'd buried along with his capacity for caring about anyone beyond himself. She'd moved on, built a life, loved someone enough to marry him and have his child. The fact that she'd lost that love only proved that life had a way of taking everything that mattered, no matter how good or deserving the person might be.

"Does she know I'm here?" He asked without even thinking. "I mean, does she know I work for you now?"

Ruby's expression softened with something that might have been sympathy. "We haven't mentioned it to her. After all, it's been twelve years since you two dated. Water under the bridge, I'm sure."

Water under the bridge. If only it were that simple. But some bridges burned so completely that the water beneath them turned to steam, leaving nothing but scorched earth and memories that refused to fade despite a man's best efforts to bury them.

"Well," he said, forcing his voice to remain steady, "I reckon I should get back to this fence..."

"Actually, Cade," Ruby interrupted, "I was hoping you'd join us for dinner tonight. I'm making pot roast. We thought it might be nice to have a nice family dinner before all the excitement of Eva's homecoming."

Family.

The word struck something in him he hadn't managed to protect, no matter how carefully he tried to armor it. The Turners had treated him like one of their own from the moment he showed up on their porch—bruised by the divorce, gutted by the loss of his family's ranch, and too proud to ask for help. Truth was, they'd considered him family long before that. Back when he and Eva were just a couple of small-town kids tangled up in first love, her parents had welcomed him in without hesitation. And even after all these years—even after he and Eva had gone their separate ways—they never once stopped treating him like a son.

"I appreciate the offer, Mrs. Turner. I surely do," he said, touching the brim of his hat in the gesture of respect his mother had drilled into him as a boy. "But I've got some bookkeeping to catch up on, and I want to check on that heifer in the south pasture before dark."

Chuck nodded, though his eyes suggested he wasn't entirely convinced by Cade's excuses. "Another time, then. But Cade—" He paused, seeming to weigh his words carefully. "Eva's been through some hard times. Lost her husband young, raised that boy on her own. She's coming home looking for a fresh start. I'd consider it a personal favor if you'd help her feel welcome."

The request carried the weight of unspoken understanding. Chuck knew about the history between Cade and his daughter, knew that their high school romance had ended when Eva left for college with dreams bigger than Riverbend Valley could contain. He was asking Cade to be the better man, to put aside whatever personal discomfort Eva's return might cause, and to help her find her footing in the community that had once been as much hers as it was his.

"Yes, sir," Cade replied, though the words felt like glass in his throat. "I'll do my best to be neighborly."

Ruby beamed at him with maternal approval. "I knew we could count on you. Eva always speaks so fondly of you whenever your name has come up in the past. I'm sure she'll be delighted to see how well you've done for yourself."

How well he'd done for himself.

The irony might have been laughable if it hadn't cut so deep. Twelve years ago, he'd worked on his family's ranch, young and confident with the future spread out before him like an unbroken horizon. Now he was a divorced man living in a cabin that belonged to someone else, with nothing to show for his adult life except calloused hands. His heart had forgotten how to hope for anything beyond getting through each day without thinking too hard about what might have been.

"Well, we'll let you get back to your work," Chuck said, laying a gentle hand on Cade's shoulder. "There's always a place at our table if you change your mind about dinner."

Cade watched them walk away, their heads bent together in quiet conversation that undoubtedly concerned him and his reaction to their daughter's homecoming. He waited until they disappeared around the corner of the barn before returning to his fence work. But the rhythm that had sustained him all afternoon was broken now, scattered like leaves in a wind that carried the scent of change.

Eva was coming home.

Tomorrow.

He drove the next fence post into the ground with more force than necessary, trying to pound away the memories that insisted on surfacing despite his best efforts to keep them buried. Eva laughing as she helped him fix this same stretch of fence during their senior year. Eva crying the night before she left for college, promising that distance wouldn't change anything between them, while they both knew it would. Eva driving off to college, leaving him standing in the dust of her departure with nothing but the promise that they'd see each other again someday when the time was right.

Well, someday had arrived, and the time felt about as wrong as it possibly could.

The smart thing would be to avoid her altogether. Lost Creek Ranch was big enough that their paths didn't have to cross that often, especially if he was careful about his timing. He could do his job, keep his head down, and let Eva rebuild her life without the complication of a broken-down cowboy.

He'd be polite if their paths crossed, neighborly as Chuck had requested, but nothing more. Eva was part of his past, and his past was a graveyard of failures he had no intention of revisiting.

Chapter 2

"**M**om, look!" Noah pressed his face against the back passenger window of their SUV, his breath fogging the glass as the Sapphire Mountains rose before them like ancient guardians welcoming them home. "The mountains are HUGE! They're like... like giant walls!"

Eva smiled, her heart lifting at the wonder in her eight-year-old son's voice. The familiar peaks had been calling to her for months, whispering promises of fresh starts and simpler living. Now, with the U-Haul trailer swaying gently behind them and everything they owned packed into eight feet of rented space, those whispers had become reality.

"They are magnificent," she agreed, slowing the vehicle as they crested the hill that offered the first panoramic view of Riverbend Valley spread out below them. The sight never failed to steal her breath—rolling pastures dotted with cattle, the silver ribbon of Deer Run River winding through the valley floor, and the town itself nestled like a precious gem among the wildflower meadows.

Noah bounced in his seat, his sandy brown hair catching the morning sunlight. "Are we really going to live here forever?"

They'd had this conversation countless times during the past month of preparations, but she understood his need for reassurance. Change was hard for anyone, but especially for a boy who'd already weathered more loss than most adults.

"This is our home now," she said firmly. "The bed and breakfast is ours, and we're going to make it beautiful again. Think of all the adventures waiting for us—helping Grandpa with the ranch, learning to ride a horse better, maybe even getting a dog like you've been asking for."

"A dog?" Noah's eyes widened with the kind of hope that made Eva's chest tighten with fierce protectiveness. "Really?"

"After we're settled in, I don't see why not," Eva confirmed, laughing at his excitement. "We'll have plenty of room for a dog."

The road curved downward after exiting the highway. They drove past the Riverbend Valley Community Church, where she'd been baptized at the age of twelve and attended youth group through high school. The white steeple reached toward heaven with faithful certainty, while the well-maintained cemetery beside it held the headstones of neighbors who'd shaped her childhood. Pastor Sam still preached there, and the familiar rhythm of Sunday mornings would provide the spiritual anchor she craved.

"Tell me again about Aunt Connie," Noah said, settling back in his seat. "Did she really bake cookies every single day?"

Eva's throat tightened with bittersweet memories. "Every afternoon. Chocolate chip on Mondays, snickerdoodles on Tuesdays, oatmeal raisin on Wednesdays..." She could almost smell the cinnamon and vanilla that had perfumed Aunt Connie's kitchen and could almost see her aunt's gentle hands kneading bread dough while sharing stories of the bed and breakfast's early days.

"And she lived all alone. She never got married... right?"

"Aunt Connie always said the bed and breakfast was her baby," Eva explained, navigating the familiar streets toward the edge of town. "She poured all her love into making it a place where people felt welcome and cared for. When I was your age, I spent a lot of time helping her with little jobs around the bed and breakfast."

They passed the Bluebird Café, where Lily Hawthorne still served the best cinnamon rolls in three counties, and then the Branding Iron Grill, where Eva had worked part-time one summer as a waitress. The buildings looked nearly the same, as if the town existed in a protective bubble where time moved more gently and change came only when it brought improvement rather than disruption.

"There it is," Eva whispered after they had driven several more miles and rounded the final curve, as the Lost Creek Bed & Breakfast came into view.

The Victorian mansion stood exactly as she remembered it. Three stories of cream-colored clapboard siding rose toward a slate roof that had weathered countless Montana storms, while the distinctive turret on the northwest corner created an elegant silhouette against the mountain backdrop. Wraparound porches on both the first and second floors provided covered spaces for morning coffee and evening conversations, their intricate gingerbread trim painted in soft sage green that complemented the natural surroundings perfectly.

"Wow," Noah breathed, unbuckling his seatbelt before Eva had even stopped the engine. "It's a castle! Can I pick my room?"

"Your room is already picked," Eva said, though her excitement matched his. The landscaping company she'd hired had maintained the property beautifully—the lawn stretched like an emerald carpet toward the creek, while Aunt Connie's perennial flower beds bloomed with early summer color that would have made her proud. "Remember? You're getting the room with the window seat that looks out toward Grandpa and Grandma's ranch."

She turned off the engine and sat for a moment, allowing the magnitude of what they'd done to settle over her like morning mist. Months ago, she'd been teaching second grade in Bozeman, counting down the days until summer break and wondering how she'd survive another year of school politics, increasing paperwork, and decreasing time actually teaching children. Today, she was moving into the bed and breakfast that sat on five acres of Montana paradise. A chance to build something meaningful for Noah's future.

"Come on, Mom!" Noah said as he opened the door and jumped out of the SUV.

Eva climbed out more slowly, her legs stiff from the long drive. The mountain air filled her lungs with the clean scent of nature, while the sound of Lost Creek babbling beyond the house provided a peaceful soundtrack that no city apartment could match.

They walked up the front steps together, Noah's hand in hers. She turned the key—Aunt Connie's key, with its old-fashioned brass fob shaped like a heart. The lock turned easily, and the door swung open to reveal the grand foyer in all its Victorian splendor.

"Oh, my," Eva whispered, stepping inside.

The cleaning service had uncovered all the furniture and restored the space to its former glory. The herringbone hardwood floors gleamed with fresh polish, while the sweeping staircase with its hand-carved banister curved gracefully upward. The stained-glass window beside the front door depicting Montana wildflowers cast rainbow patterns across the walls.

"This is where guests will check in," she told Noah, running her hand along the antique reception desk that had served the bed and breakfast for over a century. "Aunt Connie used to keep a guest book where everyone signed their names and wrote little messages about their stay."

Noah explored with the fearless curiosity of childhood, peeking into the formal parlor with its period furniture and examining the dining room where guests had gathered for breakfasts and dinners around the massive oak table. Eva followed more slowly, noting details that would need attention—the wallpaper would all come down, and the hardwood floors would benefit from professional refinishing.

But the bones of the house were magnificent, and Aunt Connie's loving care showed in every corner. Family photographs still lined the hallway, including several of Eva herself from teenage summers spent helping with the bed and breakfast.

"Mom!" Noah called from the back of the house. "This pantry is bigger than my bedroom in Bozeman!"

Eva made her way through the swinging doors that separated the kitchen from the dining room, and her breath caught at the sight of Aunt Connie's domain. The room combined vintage charm with modern convenience—white cabinets with glass fronts displayed mismatched china collected over decades, while modern appliances provided the efficiency needed for feeding multiple guests. The farmhouse sink and window above that overlooked what used to be a herb garden was perfect. The island in the center of the kitchen provided workspace that Aunt Connie had used for her daily baking marathons.

"Can we make cookies now?" Noah asked, opening cabinet doors to examine the contents.

"Not today... in a few days probably. We need to get moved in first," Eva said.

Standing in this kitchen felt like stepping into Aunt Connie's embrace, surrounded by memories of gentle lessons about hospitality, cooking, and love. The older woman had never married or had children, but she'd poured maternal affection into every guest who crossed her threshold and herself, teaching her life's most important lessons in this very room.

They continued their exploration upstairs, where six guest bedrooms waited for future visitors on the second floor. Each room reflected Aunt Connie's eye for detail—antique quilts on period beds, vases on nightstands that would hold fresh flowers, and windows that framed picture-perfect views of either the mountains or the garden. Eva made mental notes about minor updates she'd like to make—new curtains here, fresh paint there, perhaps updated bathroom fixtures that maintained the Victorian charm while providing modern comfort.

Noah's room, formerly Aunt Connie's sewing room, occupied a corner of the third floor with windows facing east toward Lost Creek Ranch. The window seat provided the perfect reading nook, while built-in shelves offered space for his growing collection of books about horses and adventure.

"Look, Mom!" He pressed his nose against the glass, pointing toward the neighboring property. "I can see Grandma and Grandpa's house! And there's the barns!"

Eva joined him at the window, her heart warming at the sight of Lost Creek Ranch spread out beyond the fence line below. The log ranch house, the complex of barns and outbuildings that supported the cattle operation, and the endless pastures where Black Angus grazed in contentment. She could see the main barn where she'd learned to ride, the holding pens where she'd helped her father sort cattle, and the foreman's cabin tucked among the trees that had housed various ranch hands throughout her childhood.

Summer memories flooded back—riding lessons with her father, helping her mother tend the vegetable garden, and picnics by the creek during family gatherings. This was the childhood she wanted for Noah, rooted in land and community and values that mattered most.

"Can we go see Grandpa and Grandma now?" Noah asked, tugging on her hand with barely contained excitement.

Eva laughed, his enthusiasm infectious. "First, we need to unhook the trailer," she said practically. "But yes, we'll go and let them know we arrived safely. Just a quick visit, though... I want to get as much unpacked as possible before dark."

"I can carry boxes," Noah offered, puffing out his thin chest with determination. "I'm strong."

"I know you are, sweetheart." Eva hugged him close, breathing in the scent of shampoo that always clung to his hair. "We're going to make this work, you know. This bed and breakfast is going to be beautiful again, and you're going to have the best childhood ever."

"A dog... that will be the best ever," Noah said with the simple confidence of eight-year-old certainty.

They made their way back downstairs, Eva's mind already organizing tasks and priorities while her heart settled into the rhythm of homecoming. The bed and breakfast would need work—fresh marketing to attract guests, minor renovations to update tired spaces, and the development of systems that would allow her to manage both hospitality and motherhood successfully. As she exited the bed and breakfast with Noah's hand in hers and the Montana mountains spread before them; Eva knew with bone-deep certainty that she'd made the right choice.

This was where they belonged. This was home.

Chapter 3

E va pulled up beside the familiar log ranch house where she'd grown up, the sight of the wraparound porch and hanging flower baskets instantly transporting her back to childhood summers filled with screen doors slamming and her mother's voice calling her in for supper. Noah was already unbuckling his seatbelt before she'd even turned off the engine, his excitement at seeing his grandparents radiating through the SUV like summer heat.

"Remember, just a quick visit," Eva reminded him as they climbed out. "We need to get back and start unpacking."

"I know," Noah said, bouncing on his toes as they approached the front steps.

Eva smiled at his enthusiasm as they climbed the porch steps and opened the front screen door.

"Mom? Dad?" she called.

Silence greeted them, except for the gentle ticking of the grandfather clock in the hallway. Eva frowned, checking her watch. Noon on a Tuesday meant her parents could be anywhere on the 3,000-acre spread, though she'd hoped to catch them during their usual lunch break.

"Maybe they're in the barn," Noah suggested, already heading back toward the door with the boundless energy that made standing still a torture for eight-year-old boys. "Come on."

Eva followed him down the porch steps and across the gravel drive toward the main barn complex. The rhythm of ranch life surrounded them—the gentle murmur of cattle in nearby pens, the rustle of wind through cottonwood leaves, and the clean scent of hay that defined her childhood memories.

The main barn's sliding doors stood open to catch the cross-breeze, revealing the shadowy interior, where feed sacks and ranch equipment created a maze of organized chaos. Eva paused in the doorway, allowing her eyes to adjust to the dimmer light, while Noah charged ahead with the fearless confidence of a boy who considered the barn his personal playground.

"Grandpa?" Noah called, his voice echoing in the cavernous space. "Grandma? Are you in here?"

A figure emerged from one of the stalls in the back, and Eva's breath caught in her throat as recognition hit her like a physical blow. Even silhouetted against the barn's far window, she knew that tall, lean frame, the way he carried himself with quiet confidence, and the careful economy of movement that had always made her think of mountain cats—graceful and powerful.

Cade Mayer.

Twelve years collapsed into nothing as he stepped into a shaft of sunlight streaming through the open doors, and Eva felt her heart stutter with the same breathless excitement that had defined her teenage years. He'd filled out since high school, his shoulders broader now, his face more angular where boyish softness had given way to masculine planes and angles. His dark hair showed threads of premature silver at the temples, and lines around his green eyes spoke of years spent squinting into Montana sun and weather that hadn't always been kind.

He was even more handsome than she remembered, and that realization hit her with a force that left her feeling unsteady.

"Eva." Her name on his lips sounded rusty, as if he hadn't spoken it aloud in years. His green eyes met hers and made her pulse quicken in ways that had nothing to do with surprise.

"Cade," she managed, her voice barely above a whisper. "Mom and Dad didn't mention..." She stopped, unable to finish the sentence while her mind raced to process his presence here, in her parents' barn, wearing work clothes that suggested he belonged here.

Noah, oblivious to the undercurrents crackling between the adults, stepped forward with the easy friendliness that made him popular with everyone, from schoolteachers to grocery store clerks. "Hi! I'm Noah! Are you a real cowboy?"

A smile tugged at the corner of Cade's mouth. "I suppose I am," he said, crouching down to Noah's eye level. "I'm Cade, your grandpa's foreman. And you must be the young man I've been hearing about—the one who's moving into the bed and breakfast next door."

"That's me!" Noah beamed, clearly delighted to be recognized. "We just got here. Mom said we can get a dog, and Grandpa's gonna teach me all about ranching."

Eva watched this exchange with a mixture of wonder and growing alarm. Noah was clearly enchanted by Cade, who listened to the boy's chatter with genuine attention rather than the polite disinterest most adults showed when children got excited. There was something in Cade's expression—a gentleness she remembered from their teenage years.

"Noah's been looking forward to spending more time on the ranch," Eva said. "He's always been drawn to..." She gestured vaguely at their surroundings, still struggling to process Cade's presence here. "To all of this."

"Smart boy," Cade said, straightening to his full height.

An uncomfortable silence stretched between them, filled with twelve years of unspoken words and the ghost of everything they'd once meant to each other. Eva found herself cataloging the changes in him—the way he held himself with a new wariness, the deeper lines around his eyes that spoke of hardship rather than laughter, and the careful distance he maintained.

"I'll radio your parents," Cade said abruptly, reaching for the walkie-talkie clipped to his belt. "Let them know you're here."

Before Eva could respond, he'd stepped away and was speaking in low tones into the device. She caught fragments—"Eva's arrived... main barn... yes, sir... yes, ma'am"—before he clipped the radio back to his belt and turned to face them again.

"They'll be here in a few minutes," he said. "Chuck was checking one of the fences near the house, and Ruby was in the garden."

"Thank you," Eva said. The formality in his voice stung more than it should have. They were strangers now, she realized. Whatever they'd once shared had been buried under years and distance and lives that had taken them in directions neither could have imagined.

"Are you really a cowboy?" Noah asked, apparently immune to the tension that seemed to thicken the barn's air. "Like, with a horse and everything?"

"I have a horse," Cade confirmed. "His name's Storm, and he's about the smartest cow pony I've ever worked with. Maybe you can meet him sometime."

"Really?" Noah's eyes went wide with the kind of hero worship that made Eva's chest tighten with protective instinct. "Could I pet him? I'm really good with horses—Grandpa taught me how to brush them and everything."

"Noah," Eva said gently. "I'm sure Mr. Mayer is very busy with his work."

"Cade," he said.

Her parents appeared in the barn doorway like a matched set of energy and excitement, her mother practically vibrating with joy, while her father wore the quiet satisfaction of a man whose family was complete again.

"Eva, honey!" Ruby said as she burst into motion the moment she spotted her daughter. "Oh, let me look at you!"

The embrace that followed was everything Eva had missed: unconditional love mixed with the scent of her mother's lavender soap and the solid reassurance of family that would never change, no matter how far she traveled or how long she stayed away. Ruby held her tight for a long moment before pulling back to study her face with the keen eyes of a mother who could read her daughter's moods like weather patterns.

"You look tired," Ruby said with gentle concern. "Was the drive difficult? And Noah—" She turned to her grandson. "Look how you've grown! You're going to be taller than your grandpa before we know it!"

Chuck's reunion was quieter but no less meaningful—a bear hug that lifted Eva off her feet, followed by his familiar rumbling laugh that had been the soundtrack of her childhood.

"Welcome home, sweetheart," he said, his voice gruff with emotion. "We've missed you."

"I've missed you too," Eva said, and meant it with her whole heart. "Both of you."

Noah had attached himself to Ruby's side and was chattering a mile a minute about the bed and breakfast, the possibility of getting a dog, and his plans for learning everything there was to know about ranch life. Eva watched her son's animated conversation with her parents, noting how naturally he fit into their world and how his excitement brought matching smiles to their faces.

From the corner of her eye, she was aware of Cade watching the reunion with an expression she couldn't quite read. When she glanced in his direction, she caught something that looked almost like longing.

"Well, this calls for a celebration," Ruby announced, clapping her hands together with the authority of a woman who'd spent decades organizing family gatherings and impromptu meals. "I've got a sliced roast beef in the slow cooker and fresh bread cooling on the counter. Everyone's coming to the house for lunch—no arguments."

"That sounds wonderful, Mom," Eva said, though she felt suddenly self-conscious about the family dynamics playing out in front of Cade. "But we really can't stay long. We need to get back and start unpacking."

"Nonsense," Ruby said with maternal firmness. "The boxes will wait, but this moment won't. It's not every day our daughter comes back home to stay."

Eva glanced toward Cade, who was already backing toward the barn's side door with the careful movements of someone trying to escape without being noticed. "I appreciate the invitation, Mrs. Turner," he said, "but I've got work to finish."

"Cade Mayer, don't you dare disappear on us," Ruby said with the tone she'd used on reluctant students for thirty years. "You're family too, and family eats together."

The word 'family' seemed to hit Cade like a physical blow. He glanced toward the door as if calculating his chances of escape, then seemed to accept defeat with the resignation of a man who'd learned not to fight battles he couldn't win.

"I wouldn't want to intrude," he said carefully, his eyes finding Eva's for just a moment before sliding away. "This is your homecoming."

"You're not intruding," Chuck said. "Now come on."

"Please come," Noah added with the innocent enthusiasm that could melt the hardest hearts. "You can tell me about Storm and being a cowboy!"

Cade looked at Noah. "Well," he said slowly, "I suppose I could spare a few minutes."

"Wonderful!" Ruby beamed, already heading toward the barn door with the brisk efficiency of a woman on a mission.

Chapter 4

Cade followed the Turner family up the front steps of the ranch house. The warm scent of home-cooked food drifted in the air as they entered, mixing with the sound of Noah's excited chatter and Ruby's gentle laughter.

"Mom said we could get a dog!" Noah was saying as they entered the kitchen, his words tumbling over each other in his enthusiasm. "A real dog!"

"Well now, that will be fun," Chuck said.

Eva moved through the kitchen with the easy grace of someone who'd grown up in this space, automatically reaching for plates from the cabinet while Ruby lifted the slow cooker lid to release a cloud of savory steam. Cade found himself watching her movements—the way she tucked a strand of hair behind her ear, the gentle efficiency with which she helped her mother, the soft smile that curved her lips as she listened to Noah's constant stream of questions and observations.

She was beautiful.

More beautiful than she'd been at eighteen, with a woman's confidence replacing the uncertainty of youth. The realization hit him like a kick from an ornery horse, sudden and unwelcome and impossible to ignore.

"Cade, sit yourself down," Ruby instructed, gesturing toward the oak table. "You know better than to hover in my kitchen."

He took a seat beside Chuck, grateful for the older man's solid presence. Noah immediately claimed the chair next to him, bouncing slightly with barely contained energy as he continued his rapid-fire commentary.

"Is Storm really smart?" Noah asked, turning those bright blue eyes—so like his mother's—toward Cade with the kind of open curiosity that made grown men want to move mountains. "Grandpa says some horses are born to work with cows."

"Storm's pretty special," Cade said. "He's been working cattle since he was three years old. Sometimes I think he knows the job better than I do."

"Can I meet him? I promise I'd be real quiet and careful."

Cade glanced toward Eva, who was setting plates around the table with movements that seemed just a fraction too controlled, as if she was working to maintain her composure. "Well," he said carefully, "that would be up to your mom."

"Mom always says yes," Noah said with eight-year-old confidence.

Eva and Ruby joined them at the table, Eva taking the seat across from Cade with a careful smile that didn't quite reach her eyes. The platters of food—tender sliced roast beef swimming in rich au jus, creamy potato salad, and thick slices of Ruby's delicious homemade bread—created a feast that spoke of love and abundance and the kind of hospitality that had always defined the Turner home.

"Chuck, would you say grace?" Ruby asked, reaching for her husband's hand with the automatic gesture of decades of shared meals and shared faith.

Cade bowed his head as Chuck's voice filled the kitchen with words of gratitude—thanks for safe travels, for family reunited, for the blessing of good food and loving fellowship. The prayer washed over him like a gentle reproach, reminding him of the faith he'd once shared with this family, the simple trust in divine providence that had sustained him through his youth and abandoned him when life proved that good intentions and honest work weren't always enough to protect the things that mattered most.

"Amen," the family chorused, and Cade found himself murmuring the word despite the doubt that had taken root in his heart like winter frost.

"So tell us about your plans for the bed and breakfast," Ruby said as she passed the potato salad, her attention focused on Eva. "Have you thought about when you'll start taking guests again?"

Eva's face lit up with genuine enthusiasm, and Cade felt something shift in his chest at the sight of her excitement. "I want to get the downstairs completely refreshed and updated first," she said, helping Noah load his plate with appropriate portions while she talked. "New curtains in the parlor, maybe some updated fixtures in the guest bathrooms, and the wallpaper definitely has to go."

"What about marketing?" Chuck asked with the practical mind of a businessman. "Folks won't know you're open unless you tell them."

"I've been researching online platforms for bed and breakfasts," Eva replied. "Plus, word of mouth had always been Aunt Connie's best advertising. Once people know we're operating again, I think the bookings will follow."

"The summer tourist season's just getting started," Cade offered, then immediately regretted speaking when all eyes turned toward him. "I mean, the hiking trails and fishing spots draw a lot of visitors through the valley during the summer. Might be good timing for reopening."

"That's something to keep in mind," Eva said, and her smile when she looked at him held none of the careful politeness she'd shown in the barn. For a moment, she was just the girl he'd once known, sharing dreams and making plans with easy confidence. "I remember how busy Aunt Connie stayed during the summer months."

"She used to complain about turning folks away," Ruby added with fond remembrance. "Said it broke her heart to disappoint people who were looking for a peaceful place to stay."

The conversation flowed around the table, touching on everything from Noah's excitement about starting a new school in the fall to Chuck's plans for rotating the cattle to fresh pasture. Cade contributed when directly addressed, but mostly he listened, absorbing the warmth and belonging that seemed to emanate from these people like heat from a well-tended fire.

This was what he'd lost when Rachel walked away—not just a wife, but the promise of this kind of life. Sunday dinners and shared laughter and children who looked at him with trust and admiration. The knowledge settled in his chest like a physical weight, reminding him of all the reasons he needed to maintain his distance from the vision of family that Eva and Noah represented.

"Are there really mountain lions here?" Noah asked suddenly as he turned to Cade, his fork suspended halfway to his mouth as his imagination clearly shifted into high gear. "Grandpa said there might be."

"There are mountain lions," Cade confirmed. "But they mostly stay away from people and livestock. As long as you stick close to the house and ranch buildings, you'll be fine."

"What about bears?" Noah pressed, his eyes wide with the delicious thrill of potential danger. "Have you ever seen a bear?"

"A few black bears over the years," Cade said, glancing toward Eva to gauge her comfort level with this conversation. "Mostly they're just looking for easy food—garbage cans, pet food left outside, that sort of thing. Nothing to worry about if you're smart about it."

"We'll be careful. No wandering off alone, young man," she said to her son.

The meal continued with Noah peppering the adults with questions about everything from cows to horses and ranch life in general, his curiosity limitless. Despite his reservations, Cade relaxed into the rhythm of family conversation, drawn in by the boy's genuine interest and Eva's gentle encouragement of her son's learning.

When the last bites had been eaten and Ruby began clearing plates, Cade pushed back his chair and stood. "I should get back to work," he said. "Thank you for lunch, Mrs. Turner. It was delicious, as always."

"No thanks needed," Ruby said with a dismissive wave. "You barely ate anything though, and we haven't had nearly enough time to catch up."

"I appreciate the hospitality," Cade said carefully, "but I've got that fence line to finish up."

He was halfway to the door when Chuck's voice stopped him. "Actually, Cade, before you go—would you mind helping Eva and Noah get their trailer unloaded?"

The request hit Cade like a trap springing shut around him.

"Dad, we don't need help," Eva said quickly, her voice carrying just a hint of strain. "Noah and I can manage fine."

Chuck was apparently oblivious to the undercurrents crackling between his foreman and his daughter. "No sense wearing yourselves out on your first day home. Cade's got a strong back and experience moving heavy things. Won't take any time at all with an extra pair of hands."

Cade looked at Eva and saw the carefully controlled expression that told him she was as uncomfortable with this arrangement as he was. The polite thing would be to decline. The smart thing would be to protect himself from the temptation she represented.

But Noah was looking at him with those bright, hopeful eyes, and Chuck was waiting for an answer with the patient expectation of a man who'd never had an employee refuse a reasonable request. And Eva, despite her obvious discomfort, needed help whether she wanted to admit it or not.

"I can spare a few hours," Cade said, though every instinct screamed that he was making a mistake. "Long as you don't mind me tracking dirt into your fancy bed and breakfast."

"That's very kind of you," she said with careful politeness. "I'm sure Noah will enjoy having someone to talk to while we work."

"I can carry boxes too!" Noah announced, bouncing up from his chair with renewed energy. "I'm strong!"

"I'm sure you are," Cade said. There was something about this boy—his enthusiasm, his genuine curiosity, his easy trust—that slipped past the defenses Cade had built around his heart like water finding cracks in stone.

Chapter 5

N oah bounced in his seat as Eva navigated the short drive from her parents' ranch to the bed and breakfast, his excitement from lunch still bubbling over. "Cade said Storm can tell when a cow's about to run! That's like magic, isn't it?"

Eva glanced in her rearview mirror at Cade's red pickup truck following behind them, her stomach doing peculiar little flips at the sight of his silhouette through the windshield. "It's not magic, sweetheart. It's experience and training, both for Cade and his horse."

"He said he would show me how to rope. Do you think he meant it?" Noah continued,

The hope in Noah's voice made Eva's chest tighten with protective instincts. Her son had been hungry for male attention since he was old enough to notice that other children had fathers, and she'd watched him latch onto various authority figures over the years—coaches, teachers, even the UPS driver, who always took time to chat when making deliveries. But there was something different about the way

Noah had responded to Cade, a natural ease that spoke of genuine connection rather than desperate seeking.

"I think Cade meant what he said," Eva replied carefully, pulling into the circular drive in front of the bed and breakfast. "But remember, he's very busy with ranch work. We can't expect him to spend a lot of time with us."

"I know," Noah said, unbuckling his seatbelt as Eva turned off the engine.

"Noah. Before we get out, I need you to remember your manners. Mr. Mayer is doing us a favor by helping with these boxes, so I want you to be polite, helpful, and careful not to get in his way. Can you do that for me?"

"Yes, ma'am. I'll be really good."

Eva took a deep breath, trying to settle the nervous energy that had been building since her dad suggested this arrangement. Through the passenger window, she watched as Cade climbed out of his truck, his movements economical and purposeful, as he approached the U-Haul trailer. He stood with his hands in his pockets, his expression neutral as he waited for them to join him, and something about his studied casualness made her suspect he was no more comfortable with this situation than she was.

They climbed out of the SUV into the warm afternoon air. The contrast between this peaceful setting and the tension crackling between the adults would have been almost amusing if Eva hadn't felt so off-balance by Cade's unexpected presence in her carefully planned new life.

"Beautiful property," Cade said as they approached, his green eyes taking in the Victorian mansion and its well-maintained grounds.

"Aunt Connie always said the mountains did most of the work," Eva replied.

Cade moved to the back of the trailer and began working the latches that secured the rear door. "Where do you want everything?" he asked, his tone businesslike and efficient.

"All the boxes are labeled," Eva said, moving closer. "Anything marked 'main bedroom' can just go in the parlor for now—I'll sort through those later. Noah's boxes go up to his room on the third floor. Kitchen items can go straight to the kitchen... that sort of thing."

"I can carry my own boxes," Noah announced, puffing out his narrow chest with determination.

"I'm sure you can," Cade said with a grin. "How about if we work as a team and carry in all your stuff together?"

The offer was made casually, but Eva didn't miss the way Noah's face lit up like Christmas morning at the prospect of being Cade's official helper. Something warm and grateful stirred in her chest at this small kindness, even as a warning voice whispered that she needed to be careful about letting Noah get too attached.

The trailer revealed the carefully packed contents of their Bozeman life—boxes of books and teaching supplies, Noah's toys and clothes, and the practical items they'd chosen to keep from eight years of building a home together. It looked like less now, packed into the confined space of the rental trailer, but Eva felt a surge of satisfaction at the thought of giving these familiar belongings new purpose in the bed and breakfast that would be their fresh start.

"This one's labeled 'Noah's adventure books,'" Cade said, hefting a medium-sized box that Noah immediately moved to steady with his small hands.

"Those are my favorites," Noah explained as they walked toward the house together. "I've got books about cowboys and explorers and kids who solve mysteries. Do you like to read?"

"When I have time," Cade replied, holding the front door open for Noah and glancing back at Eva with a look she couldn't quite interpret.

Eva followed behind them, carrying a box while listening to Noah's animated voice. Watching her son walk beside Cade, chattering easily, created a picture that was both heartwarming and dangerous.

"Up these stairs?" Cade asked as they reached the grand staircase in the foyer.

"All the way to the top," Noah said proudly, leading the way with the confidence of a boy who'd already claimed his new territory. "My room has windows so I can see Grandpa's ranch!"

Eva smiled at her son's enthusiasm. When they returned for the next load, Noah was already positioning himself as Cade's permanent helper, and Eva realized with a mixture of amusement and concern that she was becoming the third wheel in this trio.

"How long have you been working for my parents?" she asked during one of their trips to the trailer, hoping to draw Cade into conversation while Noah ran ahead to hold doors open.

"Eight months," Cade replied, selecting another box and checking its label.

"Did you always want to work in ranch management? I remember you talking about expanding your family's place when we we—"

"Plans change," Cade interrupted, his tone closing off that line of inquiry as effectively as a locked door.

They worked in relative silence after that, with Noah providing most of the conversation as he peppered Cade with questions. Eva stole glances at Cade as they carried boxes, noting the careful way he moved to avoid being near her, the patient manner in which he answered Noah's endless curiosity, and the occasional unguarded moment when something Noah said would coax a smile.

He was still handsome—more handsome than he'd been at eighteen, with the kind of weathered strength that came from years of honest work. But there was something different about him now, a careful control that suggested he was protecting himself in ways that made Eva's heart ache with questions she had no right to ask.

As they neared the end of the trailer's contents, Eva reached for one of the last boxes at the same moment Cade's hand moved toward the same target. Their fingers brushed in the confined space of the trailer, and the contact sent a jolt of electricity up her arm. It had nothing to do with static and everything to do with the memory of holding this man's hand when they were young and foolish enough to believe love could conquer anything.

"Sorry," Cade said, immediately jerking his hand away as if he'd been burned. He grabbed a different box and stepped back.

"It's fine," Eva said, as her fingers tingled from the brief contact.

The awkwardness that followed made the final few minutes of unloading stretch like taffy, with both adults being overly careful about their positioning while Noah remained blissfully oblivious to the tensions swirling around him. When the last box had been carried inside and the empty trailer sat like a discarded shell, Eva stood in the driveway with nothing left to do but say goodbye.

"Thank you," she said, tucking her hands into her pockets to resist the urge to fidget. "This would have taken us all evening without your help."

"No problem," Cade replied.

He turned toward his truck, and Eva thought that would be the end of it—a polite, distant conclusion to an afternoon that had raised more questions than it answered. But as he reached for the driver's side door handle, he paused and looked back at her with an expression that reminded her suddenly of the boy she'd once known.

"You look good, Eva," he said quietly. "Happy."

He climbed into his truck and started the engine, leaving Eva standing in the driveway with her heart racing and her mind spinning with memories. She watched his taillights disappear around the curve of the driveway and down the road that led back to Lost Creek Ranch, acutely aware of Noah beside her, waving goodbye.

The quiet, rugged man who'd just driven away bore little resemblance to the boy who'd once shared his dreams with her under Montana stars. That boy had been open and eager and unafraid of the future, while this man seemed to carry himself like he wore heavy armor.

Eva touched her fingers where they'd brushed against his, still feeling the echo of that brief contact and wondering what had happened to change someone so completely. As she turned back toward the bed and breakfast, she couldn't shake the feeling that coming back to Riverbend Valley was going to be far more complicated than she'd ever imagined.

Chapter 6

"Can we fix my room? I don't like all the flowers. Boys don't have flower rooms." Noah asked as Eva tucked him into bed. His sandy hair was still damp from his bath, and exhaustion from their full day was finally catching up with him.

Eva smiled as she perched on the edge of his narrow bed, automatically smoothing the light blanket around his small frame. She'd managed to unpack most of his belongings, and the room already looked more like it belonged to an eight-year-old boy than Aunt Connie's former workspace. His adventure books lined the built-in shelves, his collection of toy horses stood in formation on the windowsill, and his clothes were neatly arranged in the closet and folded in the dresser drawers.

"What kind of changes did you have in mind?" she asked.

"Well, maybe some pictures of horses and cows and tractors," Noah said, his words coming slower now as sleep tugged at the edges of his consciousness. "Ranch stuff."

Eva's heart squeezed at the innocent request. Noah had been surrounded by feminine influence his entire life—her teaching colleagues, her mother, even their apartment in Bozeman had reflected her preferences more than his developing identity. The ranch setting was already awakening something in him that she recognized from her own childhood.

"I think that's a great idea," she said, tucking the blanket more securely around his shoulders. "We'll go shopping soon and find some pictures and pick out a paint color you like. Maybe Grandpa has some old ranch magazines we could look through for ideas."

"And maybe Cade could tell us what a real cowboy's room looks like."

"Maybe," she said. "But first, you need to get some sleep. We have a big day tomorrow—grocery shopping, unpacking more boxes, and figuring out what else this old house needs to be ready for guests."

"Will I get to see Storm tomorrow?" Noah mumbled.

"We'll see," Eva said, pressing a gentle kiss to his forehead. "Sleep tight, sweetheart. I love you."

"Love you, Mom," he whispered, and within moments, his breathing had settled into the deep, peaceful rhythm of childhood sleep.

Eva stood for a moment, quietly watching her son's face relax completely. She slipped out of Noah's room, leaving the door cracked open the way he preferred, and made her way downstairs. The Keurig that she'd unpacked and set up on the counter looked too modern against the vintage charm of the room, but Aunt Connie would have appreciated the convenience. Eva selected a medium roast pod and listened to the familiar gurgling that promised caffeine and a few moments of quiet reflection. The day had been overwhelming in ways she hadn't anticipated—not just the physical work of moving and unpacking, but the emotional complexity of seeing Cade again, of watching Noah respond to him with such natural enthusiasm, of feeling her heart react to her first love.

Coffee mug in hand, Eva retrieved a notebook and pen from the kitchen drawer where she had put them, then made her way through the house to the front porch. The wraparound veranda provided the perfect spot for contemplation, with wicker furniture that invited lingering and mountain views that never failed to inspire gratitude for the beauty of this place.

The evening air carried the scent of pine and the distant sound of cattle settling for the night, while stars danced in the vast Montana sky. Eva settled into one of the cushioned chairs and opened her notebook to a fresh page, determined to organize her thoughts and priorities into manageable tasks.

Tomorrow - Wednesday:

Grocery shopping - full restock

Unpack kitchen boxes completely

Call insurance company about updating policy

Research local suppliers for B&B linens

Check all guest room light fixtures

The practical list grounded her in the immediate reality of building a business and creating a home for Noah. But as she sipped her coffee and gazed across the property toward Lost Creek Ranch, her mind began to wander down other paths.

They had both been seventeen when they'd started dating during their junior year of high school. Cade had been all lanky height and easy grins and dreams that seemed as vast as the Montana sky above her. She could still remember the first time he'd kissed her.

He'd been different then—open and eager and utterly convinced that hard work and honest intentions could overcome any obstacle. They'd spent countless hours together, talking about their plans for the future with the confidence of teenagers who believed love could conquer anything.

Senior year had been bittersweet, filled with fun and adventure, growing closer, and making plans for their futures. In the end, Cade had never asked her to stay, had never made her feel guilty for choosing Montana State University over a closer community college that would have kept her close to home. Instead, he'd encouraged her dreams, even when they both knew those dreams would take her away from him. He had helped her study for college entrance exams even when the results would separate them. He had loved her with the generous heart of a boy who wanted her happiness more than his own.

The breakup, when it finally came the week before she left for college, had been gentle and mutual and devastating in its maturity. They'd both known that trying to maintain a long-distance relationship would only prolong the inevitable, that she needed to explore the world beyond Riverbend Valley while he needed to focus on building the life that called to him here. But knowing something was right didn't make it hurt any less, and Eva could still remember the way Cade had hugged and kissed her goodbye, his voice rough with unshed tears as he'd whispered that he'd always love her.

She'd written to him during her freshman year, long letters filled with descriptions of college life. His responses had come less frequently over time and with diminishing length until eventually they'd stopped altogether. She'd told herself it was for the best, that clean breaks healed faster than wounds kept fresh by constant contact.

Then she'd met David during her junior year of college, steady and kind and entirely different from the boy she'd left behind in Riverbend

Valley. David had been safe and predictable and ambitious and content with life, far from the ranch and the mountains and the memories that belonged to her past.

Their marriage had been good, built on compatibility and shared goals and the kind of mature love that grew from friendship. David had understood her need to stay connected to her family back here at home, had encouraged her visits home, and talked about retiring to a place like Riverbend Valley someday when their teaching careers were complete. He would have supported her decision to move home if he'd lived and would have probably embraced the adventure of running a bed and breakfast with the same quiet enthusiasm he'd brought to every other challenge they'd faced together.

But David was gone, taken by a heart defect that no one had known existed until it was too late. She was sitting on the front porch of the bed and breakfast, thinking about a man she'd once loved and wondering what kind of heartbreak had changed him from the eager boy she remembered into the guarded stranger who'd helped move her boxes with careful politeness. He had looked at her like she was a puzzle he couldn't solve.

Eva shook her head, deliberately closing the notebook and pushing away the memories that served no purpose except to complicate a situation. Cade was part of her past, not her future, and dwelling on what had been—or what might have been if circumstances had been different—would only distract her from the goals she'd come here to achieve.

She had a business to rebuild, a son to raise, and a life to construct from the pieces of her old dreams and her new reality. The bed and breakfast needed her full attention if it was going to succeed, and Noah deserved a mother who was focused on their future rather than haunted by ghosts from her teenage years.

Rising from her chair, Eva took one last look across the property toward the lights of Lost Creek Ranch, where Cade was probably settling into his evening routines in the foreman's cabin. Tomorrow she would concentrate on groceries and unpacking and all the practical details that would transform this house into a home.

The past was behind her, no matter how unexpectedly it had appeared in the form of a quiet cowboy with green eyes and a smile that could still make her heart skip beats. Her future lay in the Victorian mansion, in the son sleeping peacefully upstairs, and in the dream of creating something beautiful and lasting in the place where she'd always belonged.

That was enough. It had to be enough.

Chapter 7

The laptop screen cast a soft glow across Cade's hands as he scrolled through the feed supply order, double-checking quantities against his handwritten notes.

He took a sip of black coffee from the chipped ceramic mug that had seen better days, reviewing the list one more time before confirming the order. Two tons of alfalfa hay, mineral supplements for the breeding stock, and replacement parts for the water tank system that had been acting up. Practical, necessary items that would keep the ranch running smoothly—the kind of details that Chuck trusted him to handle.

The cursor hovered over the submit button as Cade's concentration wavered, his mind drifting despite his efforts to focus on the mundane task at hand. The afternoon had been more complicated than any workday had a right to be, filled with memories and emotions.

He clicked submit and watched the confirmation screen appear, knowing he'd drive into town tomorrow to pick up the order from

Morrison's Feed and Supply. Another day, another list of tasks designed to keep his hands busy and his thoughts occupied. It was a system that had worked well enough until Eva had walked back into his life with her eight-year-old son, who looked at him like he hung the moon.

Cade closed the laptop and set it aside, leaning back in the wooden rocker. Across the pasture, lights glowed warmly in the windows of the Lost Creek Bed & Breakfast, and he could barely make out a figure moving around inside the kitchen.

The sight stirred memories he'd spent twelve years trying to forget. Memories of their high school years. He'd been so sure of everything then, so confident that hard work and honest intentions could overcome any obstacle life might throw at them. He had been so sure that his love for her would eventually bring her back to him after she graduated from college.

The breakup had been mutual. He remembered the conversation clearly, sitting on the tailgate of his truck under a canopy of stars while they both struggled with words that needed to be said.

"We both know this is right," Eva had said, her voice thick with tears. "I need to focus on college, and you need to focus on the ranch that you'll own someday. We can't build our futures if we're always looking backward."

He'd agreed because it was what she needed to hear, because he could see the conflict tearing her apart between her love for him and her dreams of something bigger than Riverbend Valley could offer. But in his heart, he'd wanted to fight for her, wanted to ask her to stay or promise to wait or find some way to bridge the distance that college would create between them.

Instead, he'd kissed her goodbye and told her he agreed, and watched her drive away the next week with a smile on his face and a hole in his chest that had taken years to stop aching. He'd convinced himself it was the noble thing to do—setting her free to discover who she was meant to become, without him holding her back.

The irony wasn't lost on him now. He'd given her up to protect her future, only to have his own future destroyed by another woman who'd seen his love as a convenience rather than a gift.

A soft whinny from the direction of the barn reminded him that Storm would need attention in the morning, and the familiar thought of his horse brought a small measure of comfort. At least some relationships could be trusted to remain steady and true, built on mutual respect and shared purpose rather than the shifting sands of human emotion.

His mind drifted to Noah, and Cade caught himself smiling at the memory of the boy's endless questions and boundless enthusiasm. There was something pure about Noah's excitement, untainted by the disappointments that taught adults to guard their hearts. The kid was a character, all right—smart and curious and hungry for the kind of male guidance that Eva couldn't provide despite her obvious devotion.

That hunger worried him, though. Noah was clearly starved for masculine attention, and Cade had seen enough fatherless boys over the years to know how easily they could latch onto any available male figure. The last thing Eva needed was her son getting attached to a man who had nothing to offer except broken dreams and a bitter understanding of how quickly life could strip away everything that mattered.

The thought of Noah led inevitably to thoughts of Rachel, and Cade felt the tightness in his chest that accompanied any memory of his ex-wife. Even now, months after the divorce was finalized, the betrayal felt fresh—not just the affair, though that had been devastating enough, but the calculated way she'd dismantled his life with the help of her lover.

He'd loved Rachel and thought he'd seen in her the promise of a family he'd always wanted to build on the land his grandfather had fought to keep during the Depression. She'd seemed to love the ranch at first and had talked about raising children who would grow up understanding the value of hard work and connection to the land. But somewhere along the way, that love had curdled and changed, and the isolation that Cade found peaceful had become a prison she was desperate to escape.

The affair had been going on for months before he'd discovered it—a lawyer from Billings she happened to meet one day while out shopping in the city. Looking back, Cade could see the signs he'd missed: the trips to town that lasted longer than necessary, the phone calls that ended abruptly when he entered the room, the growing criticism of ranch life, and increasing pressure for him to consider other career options.

The divorce itself had been swift. Rachel's lover—now her husband—had structured the settlement with surgical precision, knowing exactly which assets to target to cause maximum damage. The family ranch, already carrying debt from improvements Cade had made in hopes of expanding the operation, became impossible to maintain once the settlement terms required him to buy out Rachel's share of the property.

Selling the ranch had felt like cutting out his heart. Three generations of Mayer family history, reduced to a check that barely covered his debts after the lawyers took their fees. He'd been left with his truck, his horse, his personal belongings, and the bitter knowledge that the woman he thought he had loved had systematically destroyed everything his family had built.

The experience had made him question everything he'd believed about himself as a man, as a provider, and as someone worthy of love and loyalty. If he couldn't even keep his own wife happy, what did that say about his capacity to build the kind of lasting relationship that formed the foundation of a meaningful life?

The months after the divorce had been the darkest of his life, filled with self-doubt and a rage that he'd been afraid to examine too closely. He'd drifted from job to job, unable to settle anywhere that reminded him of what he'd lost, until Chuck Turner had offered him the foreman position at Lost Creek Ranch with the kind of quiet understanding that had probably saved his sanity.

Working for Chuck and Ruby had given him purpose again, had reminded him that he was good at what he did, even if he'd failed spectacularly at marriage. The Turners had always treated him like family, including him in Sunday dinners and holiday celebrations, with the generous hearts of people who understood that loneliness could be as devastating as any physical injury. But even their kindness came with boundaries—he was the employee, not a son, and there were parts of their lives where he would always be an outsider looking in.

That knowledge had been easier to accept before Eva came home. Now, watching the warm lights of the bed and breakfast and knowing she was there, Cade knew he had to be careful. He'd be lying to himself if he denied his attraction to her wasn't still there. She was more beautiful now than she'd been at eighteen. His resurfaced feelings for her seemed deeper now. A recognition of everything he'd once wanted and still craved, despite the bitter lessons life had taught him about the cost of wanting too much.

Eva deserved better than a broken-down cowboy who'd proven he couldn't protect the things that mattered most. She deserved someone who could offer her the security and stability she needed to build the life she wanted for herself and Noah. Someone who hadn't been hollowed out by betrayal and left with nothing but scars where his faith in love used to live.

The smart thing—the only thing—to do was to maintain a careful distance. Be polite when their paths crossed and helpful when Chuck asked him to assist with something related to her or the bed and breakfast. But never close enough to risk the kind of connection that could hurt them both when it inevitably fell apart.

Cade drained the last of his coffee and stood, gathering his laptop. He allowed himself one last look at those distant lights in the bed and breakfast, then turned his back on them and headed inside. The emptiness of the cabin waited on him like an old friend who never asked questions or expected more than he had to give.

Some men were meant for love and family and the kind of dreams that required faith in tomorrow. Others were meant to work in the shadows of other people's happiness, finding what satisfaction they could in useful labor and the knowledge that they were competent enough to be trusted with important tasks.

Cade had learned which category he belonged to, and no amount of wishful thinking could change the fundamental truth of his limitations. The sooner he accepted that Eva's return was just another test of his ability to keep his heart safely locked away, the sooner he could get back to the business of surviving one day at a time.

Chapter 8

The fence post gave way with a satisfying crack as Cade worked, sweat beading on his forehead despite the morning coolness that still clung to the Montana air. He'd been working this section of fence line since dawn, replacing rotted posts along the border between Lost Creek Ranch and the bed and breakfast property—a task that required his full attention and provided the perfect excuse to avoid thinking about the woman who'd moved in next door.

Storm grazed peacefully about ten yards away, his reins draped over his neck as he took advantage of the tender grass that grew thick along the creek bottom. The bay gelding was content to follow along at his own pace while Cade moved from post to post.

The morning sun caught the dew on the pasture grass, creating millions of tiny diamonds that would disappear as soon as the day warmed properly. It was the kind of Montana morning that reminded a man why he'd chosen a life in this valley, surrounded by mountains that seemed to touch heaven and land that had been worked by honest hands for generations. The kind of morning that made the loss of his own ranch ache like an old injury before bad weather.

Cade was positioning the new post when a young voice piped up, cheerful and curious in the way that only eight-year-old boys could manage before the world taught them to be more cautious with their enthusiasm.

"Is that Storm?"

Cade found Noah about fifteen feet away, studying the horse with intense fascination. The kid was dressed in jeans and a t-shirt that proclaimed him a "Future Rancher," and his sandy hair stuck up in cowlicks.

"He's a handsome feller, all right," Cade agreed, wiping his hands on his jeans. His first instinct was to look around for Eva, wondering if she knew her son had wandered over to the fence line.

"Can Storm really run cattle?" Noah asked, his blue eyes—so much like his mother's—bright with curiosity. "I mean, without you telling him what to?"

Storm lifted his head at the sound of his name, grass hanging from his mouth as he regarded the boy with the patient tolerance of a horse who knew children were generally harmless. The gelding's ears pricked forward with interest, and after a moment's consideration, he ambled closer to the fence while Noah climbed the fence rails and threw one leg over, balancing on the top rail.

"Most of the time," Cade said, unable to suppress a smile. "Storm's been working cattle since he was three years old. After a while, a good cow horse learns to read the herd better than most cowboys do. He knows when a steer's thinking about bolting before the steer knows it."

"That's magic," Noah breathed, reaching out tentatively toward Storm's velvet nose as the horse approached the fence. "Mom says it's training, but it seems like magic to me."

"Your mom's not wrong," Cade said, moving closer to supervise the interaction between boy and horse. "But the magic part isn't wrong, either. Some horses just have a natural instinct for cattle work, the same way some people have a natural instinct for music or math. Storm was born knowing how to work with cows—I just helped him figure out how to do it better."

Noah's face lit up as Storm allowed him to stroke the white blaze that ran down the center of his face. The horse stood perfectly still, seeming to understand that this was an important moment for the boy, and Cade felt something warm and unexpected unfurl in his chest at the sight of Noah's wonder.

"Could you teach me to ride like a real cowboy?" Noah asked, his voice carrying the kind of hope that could break a grown man's heart if he wasn't careful. "I know how to ride a little bit—Grandpa taught me. I wanna do real cowboy stuff."

The question hit Cade hard. He'd always imagined teaching his own children to ride, passing down the skills his father and grandfather had taught him, watching small hands learn to hold reins and small bodies learn to move with a horse's rhythm. The fact that those children would never exist—that his capacity to be a father had been destroyed along with everything else Rachel had taken from him—was a wound that would never heal.

"That's something you'd need to talk to your mom about," Cade said. "Learning to be a cowboy takes a lot of practice, and you need to be comfortable in the saddle."

"But you could teach me, right?" Noah pressed. "I mean, if Mom says it's okay?"

As Cade tried to formulate an answer, the sound of hurried footsteps announced someone's approach. He looked up to see Eva jogging toward them, her expression a mixture of relief and exasperation that he remembered from his childhood, when his mother had discovered him somewhere he wasn't supposed to be.

"Noah Alexander Blankenship," Eva called out as she approached. "What have I told you about leaving the house without telling me where you're going?"

Noah's face fell as he realized he was in trouble, his shoulders sagging with the dejection of a boy who'd been caught breaking rules. "Sorry, Mom. I just saw Cade, and I wanted to meet Storm. Look, I can still see the house... I'm safe—"

"And you should have asked first," Eva interrupted firmly. "You can't just disappear, sweetheart. I was worried sick when I couldn't find you."

She turned to Cade, and he felt that jolt of awareness that seemed to accompany every interaction with her. She was wearing jeans and a soft blue t-shirt that brought out the color of her eyes, and her hair was pulled back in a ponytail that made her look younger than her thirty years. There were worry lines around her eyes that spoke of the stress of single motherhood, but also a warmth and strength that drew him like a moth to a flame.

"I'm so sorry," she said, her cheeks flushed with embarrassment. "I hope he wasn't bothering you. He's been talking nonstop about meeting Storm since yesterday, but I've told him he needs to wait for permission before—"

"He's no bother," Cade interrupted, surprised by how much he meant it.

Eva's expression softened, and Cade caught a glimpse of the girl she'd been in high school—the one who'd believed the best of everyone and had looked at him like he hung the moon.

"Can I pet him one more time?" Noah asked hopefully.

Eva looked at Cade questioningly, and he found himself nodding. "Storm doesn't mind the attention," he said. "He's about as gentle as they come."

Noah's face brightened as he reached out to stroke the horse's neck again, his small hands confident as he ran his fingers through Storm's dark mane. The horse leaned into the attention with obvious enjoyment, and Cade had to admit they made a picture—the eager boy and the patient horse.

"Are you fixing the fence?" Noah asked. His attention had shifted to the tools scattered around Cade's work area, and he was studying the post puller with the fascination of an engineer examining a new invention. "That thing looks real strong. "

"It's got enough leverage to remove posts that have been in the ground for decades," Cade confirmed. "The trick is getting the chain positioned just right, so you're pulling straight up instead of at an angle."

"Could you show me?" Noah asked, slipping down from the fence rail with the quick movement of a boy who'd spotted an opportunity for something fun.

Cade glanced at Eva, who was watching the interaction with an expression he couldn't quite read. There was wariness there, the protective instinct of a mother.

"It's not really something for—" Cade began, then stopped as he saw Noah's face fall. "Well, I suppose I could show you how it works."

Eva moved closer as Cade showed Noah how to position the chain around the base of an already-loosened post, explaining the principles of leverage in easy terms for the boy to understand. The boy listened with the intense concentration, asking questions and following instructions with surprising precision for an eight-year-old.

"Pull steady, don't jerk," Cade instructed as he helped Noah grip the handle of the post puller. "Let the tool do the work."

The post came free with a satisfying pop, and Noah's whoop of triumph was loud enough to startle a bird from a nearby bush. "I did it! Did you see that, Mom? I pulled out a whole fence post!"

"I saw," Eva said. "Very impressive."

Cade watched Eva's face as she observed Noah's joy, noting the way her expression softened when she looked at her son and the obvious pride she took in his accomplishments. There was something beautiful about her devotion to the boy.

"And now a new post in the hole?" Noah asked, already moving toward the replacement post.

"After we make sure it's the right depth, tamp down the soil. Fence posts have to be set deep enough to hold against wind and cattle pushing against them."

They worked together for the next few minutes, with Noah providing eager assistance and running commentary, while Cade guided the new post into position. Eva watched with the expression of a mother who was seeing her child discover something that brought him genuine happiness.

"Best day ever," Noah announced as they finished tamping soil around the base of the new post. "I helped fix a real fence... and I got to pet Storm. Wait 'til I tell Grandpa!"

"Speaking of Grandpa," Eva said gently, "we should probably let Cade get back to his work. He's got a lot of fences to repair, and we're keeping him from it."

Cade wanted to protest that he didn't mind the company, that Noah's enthusiasm had made the morning's work more enjoyable than any he'd done in months. But Eva was right—he had a job to do, and lingering here with her and Noah was dangerous territory.

"Could I... could I maybe help again sometime?" Noah asked.

The hope in the boy's voice was almost painful to hear.

"We'll see," he said finally.

Noah nodded solemnly, apparently recognizing that "we'll see" was better than an outright refusal.

"Thank you," Eva said. "He... he hasn't had many opportunities to do things like this. I appreciate your patience with him."

There was gratitude mixed with a wistfulness in her voice.

"He's a good kid. Smart, too."

Eva's smile was soft and proud, and Cade felt that dangerous warmth spreading through his chest again. She was a good mother—patient and loving and clearly devoted to giving Noah the best childhood she could manage on her own. The fact that she was doing it all without help spoke to a strength and determination that he couldn't help but admire.

"I should let you get back to your work," she said, breaking the spell that had settled over them. "I've got a million errands to run, and I need to figure out what we're having for dinner this evening besides peanut butter and jelly sandwiches."

"Grocery shopping day?"

"Definitely," Eva said with a rueful laugh.

"Morrison's is still your best bet for groceries," Cade said automatically. "They've got everything you need, and the prices are fair."

Eva nodded.

She turned to follow Noah, who was already making his way back to the house, chattering excitedly about fence posts and horses and the wonders of ranch life. Cade watched them go.

As Eva and Noah disappeared around the corner of the bed and breakfast, Cade returned his attention to the fence line. But his concentration was shot now, his mind replaying the morning's interaction and the way Noah had looked at him with such obvious hero worship.

He'd been kidding himself if he thought he could maintain a complete distance from his new neighbors.

Chapter 9

Eva pushed open the door to the Bluebird Café, Noah bouncing beside her. The scent of fresh coffee and diner food enveloped them like a warm hug, instantly transporting Eva back to countless afternoons during her teenage years when she'd stopped by after school for one of Lily Hawthorne's famous treats and the latest town gossip.

"Mom, this place smells like heaven," Noah announced with the unfiltered honesty that made eight-year-olds such delightful companions. "Do they have hamburgers? I'm hungry!"

Eva laughed, ruffling his already-disheveled hair as they paused in the doorway to take in the cozy interior. The Bluebird Café hadn't changed a bit—the same blue and white checkered tablecloths adorned mismatched antique tables, local photography showcasing Montana's natural beauty lined the walls, and the display case near the counter held an array of tempting baked goods. The lunch rush was just beginning, with several tables occupied by ranchers, business owners, and retirees who treated the café as their unofficial daily meeting place.

"Well, if it isn't Eva Turner!" a warm voice called out from behind the counter, and Eva's heart lifted at the sight of Lily Hawthorne's smile that could power the entire valley. At fifty-one, Lily possessed the kind of timeless beauty that came from a life spent making others happy—laugh lines around her gentle blue-gray eyes, silver threading heavily through her hair, and the confident bearing of a woman who'd found her calling in feeding people's bodies and souls.

"It's Eva Blankenship now," Eva corrected gently, moving toward the counter with Noah trailing behind, his attention already captured by the impressive array of pies and cookies in the display case. "It's good to see you, Lily. You haven't changed a bit."

"Flatterer," Lily said with a delighted laugh, coming around the counter to envelop Eva in a bear hug. "Though I'll take all the compliments I can get at my age. And this handsome young man must be Noah!"

Noah looked up from his intense study of a chocolate cake that defied the laws of physics with its impressive height, offering Lily a shy smile. "Yes, ma'am. Mom said you make the best cinnamon rolls."

"Your mama always was a smart girl," Lily said, winking at Eva. "Tell me, Noah, are you planning on helping your mom get the bed and breakfast running again? That's going to be quite an adventure."

"Yes," Noah said with the confidence of youth, his chest puffing out slightly with pride. "I have my own room... and we're getting a dog... and I'm gonna be a cowboy...and Cade let me fix a fence post with this really cool thing that uses lev... lev... rage..., and—"

"Slow down there, cowboy," Eva interrupted gently, placing a hand on Noah's shoulder before his enthusiasm could carry him into a monologue that might last until dinner. "Let's find a table and order some lunch before you tell Lily your whole life story."

Lily's expression brightened. "Cade Mayer? He's working for your folks, right? He's such a good man... he sure has had a rough time of it lately."

Something in Lily's tone suggested there was more to that story, but Eva wasn't sure how much she wanted to know.

"Let's grab that corner table," Eva said, steering the conversation toward safer territory while guiding Noah toward a spot near the window that offered a view of Main Street's afternoon bustle. "Noah's wanting a hamburger."

"My burgers are the best in the valley," Lily said, following them to the table with menus in hand and the graceful efficiency of someone who'd spent decades managing a busy restaurant. "And the fries are still hand-cut fresh every morning. Though if you're looking for something lighter, the chicken salad sandwich is popular with the ladies who lunch."

Noah immediately buried himself with the menu, his lips moving silently as he sounded out words he didn't already know. Eva settled into her chair, grateful for the comfort of the café and the genuine warmth of Lily's welcome.

"I can't believe you're really back to stay," Lily said, settling into the third chair at their table with the casual familiarity of an old friend. "Your parents have been so excited about this move. Ruby stops by at least twice a week for coffee, and she could barely contain herself last week talking about having you and Noah close by again."

"It feels surreal," Eva admitted, glancing around the café that held so many memories of her teenage years. "But good. Really good. Noah needs this—the space to run and explore, the chance to learn about ranch life and the stability of family close by. And I need it too, more than I can possibly explain."

"Teaching wasn't working out?" Lily asked with the gentle curiosity.

"The politics were getting overwhelming. More time is spent on paperwork and testing than actually teaching children. I love working with kids, but the ever-evolving system built around education was sucking all the joy out of it. It was time for a change."

"Your aunt Connie would be so proud of you," Lily said softly, her expression growing wistful. "She always knew you'd take over the bed and breakfast one day. She poured her heart into that place for so many years, creating a little piece of paradise for anyone who needed refuge from the world."

"And I'm going to continue that," Eva said, feeling the spark of excitement that came from talking about her dreams for the property. "A place where people can disconnect from the stress of modern life and remember what really matters. Good food, comfortable beds, and the kind of peace that only comes from being surrounded by Montana's natural beauty."

"Mom's gonna make cookies every day," Noah chimed in. "And maybe we can do campfires with s'mores!"

"That sounds like a good idea," Lily said, her smile encompassing both mother and son with obvious approval.

Their conversation was interrupted by the arrival of a middle-aged couple, who approached their table with warm smiles and the comfortable bearing of people who belonged to this community as surely as the mountains belonged to the landscape. Eva recognized them immediately—Pastor Sam Harlow and his wife, Virginia.

"Eva Blankenship!" Pastor Sam's voice boomed with genuine delight as he extended his hand in greeting. "I heard through the church grapevine that you were moving home. Welcome home, child... welcome home!"

Eva stood to accept his handshake, which immediately transformed into one of his famous bear hugs that had comforted countless parishioners through good times and difficult ones. At forty-eight, Sam Harlow possessed the rare combination of spiritual authority and approachable warmth that made him beloved by believers and skeptics alike. Virginia's gentle nature and genuine interest in people's wellbeing had made her an integral part of the church community's fabric.

"It's wonderful to see you both," Eva said, meaning every word. "This is my son Noah—you met him last summer when we visited for Mom and Dad's anniversary."

Noah stood and offered his hand to both adults with the manners Eva had worked hard to instill in him. "Nice to meet you," he said quietly, though his eyes brightened when Virginia smiled at him with the kind of genuine warmth that put children immediately at ease.

"Oh my, you have grown," Virginia said. "Are you excited about living so close to your grandparent's ranch?"

"Yes, ma'am!" Noah's shyness evaporated in the face of a topic that never failed to capture his full attention. "This morning I helped Cade fix a fence... I met his horse, Storm... he's gonna show me how to be a cowboy."

"How is Cade doing?" Pastor Sam asked, his tone carefully neutral. "He'd been having a difficult time..."

"Since his divorce," Lily filled in quietly, her voice carrying the sympathy of someone who'd witnessed the aftermath of that particular life upheaval. "Lost everything, poor man. The ranch, his marriage, and his faith in just about everything good in this world. Your parents hiring him was such a blessing."

The words hit Eva like a physical blow, explaining so much about the guarded, careful man she'd encountered yesterday—so different from the open, optimistic boy she'd once known. Learning that he'd lost not just his marriage but his family's ranch created a hollow ache in her chest that she wasn't prepared to examine too closely.

"Oh my," Virginia said softly, apparently noticing Eva's reaction to this news. "I'm sorry, dear. I assumed you knew about his circumstances."

"No... I didn't. We haven't had much chance to catch up on... personal matters."

The truth was more complicated than that simple statement suggested. Yesterday's brief interactions with Cade had revealed glimpses of the pain he carried, but she'd attributed his guardedness to the natural awkwardness of encountering an old girlfriend. Learning that he'd been through a divorce and lost his family's ranch put his careful distance in an entirely different light.

"Well, working for your daddy is the best thing that could have happened to him," Pastor Sam said. "Cade's a good man, and ranch work is honest work. Sometimes that's exactly what a person needs to start healing."

"Cade's really nice," Noah interjected. "He said I could help with ranch work."

Eva felt her protective instincts stirring at Noah's obvious interest in Cade. It was one thing for her son to be fascinated by ranch life and eager to learn from the cowboys who worked her father's land. It was another thing entirely for him to form an emotional bond with a man who was clearly dealing with his own significant problems and might not be in a position to provide the stable masculine influence Noah craved and needed.

"That's very kind of him," she said carefully, reaching over to smooth Noah's hair in an unconsciously protective gesture. "But remember, Mr. Mayer has important work to do for Grandpa."

"I know… but he said I'm smart. That means I'm good at ranch stuff, right?"

The pride in Noah's voice was unmistakable, and Eva felt her heart squeeze.

"You're good at lots of things," she said. "Ranch work is just one of many skills you'll be able to explore."

"Speaking of exploring," Lily interjected, "think about enrolling Noah in our summer youth programs at church? We have activities several days a week that give kids a chance to make friends and have fun."

"That sounds wonderful," Eva said, grateful for the change of subject. "It would be great for Noah to meet some kids in the area before school starts in the fall."

"There's also 4-H," Virginia added enthusiastically. "Several of the ranch families participate, and it's a great way for kids to learn while working with animals. They have everything from livestock projects to photography and cooking competitions."

Noah's eyes lit up at the mention of working with animals, and Eva could practically see the wheels turning in his head. "Could I do that, Mom? Please? I promise I'd be really good."

"We'll look into it," Eva said. "Let's get settled in our new home first, then we can explore some of these things."

"That's wise," Pastor Sam said approvingly. "Moving is stressful enough without taking on too many new commitments all at once. Though I hope we'll see you both in church this Sunday."

"We'll be there," Eva promised.

Lily pulled out her notepad, ready to take their lunch orders. The discussion shifted to Noah ultimately deciding on a cheeseburger and fries after much deliberation, while Eva opted for the chicken salad sandwich that Lily had recommended.

After Pastor Sam and Virginia excused themselves to return to their meals and afternoon responsibilities, Eva found herself thinking about this community, where people knew your name and cared about your well being. The easy warmth of Lily's welcome, the genuine affection of Pastor Sam and Virginia, and the knowledge that Noah would grow up surrounded by people who would watch out for him and celebrate his accomplishments created a feeling of security.

"Mom," Noah said. "I like it here. Everyone's so nice."

"That's what small towns are like," Eva explained. "People care about each other and look out for one another. It's different from the city, where you might not even know your neighbors' names."

"I like it," Noah declared with the certainty of youth. "And I like that Cade lives right next door."

"Remember, Mr. Mayer has an important job on Grandma and Grandpa's ranch. We can't expect him to be available whenever you want."

"I know," Noah said with the long-suffering patience of a child who'd heard this particular lecture multiple times. "But maybe sometimes we can go over there and see if he's busy."

Eva nodded noncommittally, unwilling to make promises.

Chapter 10

Eva perched on the stepladder, carefully scoring another section of stubborn wallpaper, the aged floral pattern that had adorned Aunt Connie's dining room for the past twenty years finally surrendering. The adhesive remover filled the air with its sharp chemical scent, mixing with the sounds of her mother's cheerful humming and the satisfying zip of wallpaper coming free from the walls.

"I think this wallpaper was installed with superglue," Eva said to her mom, who was working on the lower portion of the same wall with methodical patience.

Ruby laughed, the sound filling the dining room that looked like a tornado had swept through it. Drop cloths covered every piece of furniture, plastic sheeting protected the hardwood floors, and garbage bags bulging with stripped wallpaper stood like sentinels around the room's perimeter. The kitchen wallpaper had been removed yesterday, leaving the room looking fresh and bright, and Eva was eager to continue the momentum with the dining room transformation.

"Your Aunt Connie always said that if something was worth doing, it was worth doing right," Ruby said, attacking a particularly stubborn corner with the wallpaper scraper. "She probably used enough adhesive to hold together the Brooklyn Bridge, bless her heart."

The morning had started early, with Noah bouncing off the walls with excitement about spending the day helping his grandpa with ranch work, while Eva and Ruby tackled the wallpaper removal project. Chuck had arrived at nine o'clock sharp to collect his grandson, and the sight of Noah's face lighting up when he spotted his grandfather's truck in the driveway had warmed Eva's heart.

"Pass me that spray bottle," Eva said, gesturing toward the arsenal of wallpaper removal supplies they'd assembled on the floor surrounding them.

At fifty-two, Eva's mother possessed the kind of timeless energy that came from a life spent nurturing students, family, and community members with equal devotion. Her graying hair was pulled back in a clip, and she wore old jeans and one of Chuck's work shirts that bore the evidence of their morning's labor.

"You know," Ruby said, returning to her scraping with renewed vigor, "I'm so tickled with everything you're doing in this house. Taking on this project, moving back home, giving Noah the chance to grow up near the ranch... I'm just so overwhelmingly proud of you and your courage."

"Some days it feels more like insanity than courage," Eva admitted, carefully peeling away another strip of wallpaper. "Especially when I'm looking at how much work this place needs and wondering if I've bitten off more than I can chew."

"Nonsense," Ruby said. "You've got good instincts, a strong work ethic, and more determination than any one person should reasonably possess. This bed and breakfast will be beautiful again in no time, and you're precisely the person to make it happen."

The vote of confidence warmed Eva's heart as she moved the ladder to tackle the next section of wall. "I'm thinking about keeping the wallpaper in the guest rooms upstairs—it's in good condition and fits the Victorian atmosphere perfectly. But down here, I want something fresher and more welcoming for the common areas."

"What are you thinking for color schemes?" Ruby asked, stepping back to survey their progress.

"Soft, warm colors that complement each other," Eva said, visualizing the finished result even as she wrestled with another stubborn section of adhesive. "Maybe sage green in here with cream trim and a warm butter yellow for the parlor. Colors that feel peaceful and inviting without overwhelming the natural beauty visible through the windows."

"That sounds perfect," Ruby agreed. "And what about Noah's room? He's been talking nonstop about his decorating plans ever since you mentioned he could change it."

Eva's face lit up. "We're planning a trip to one of the big box stores soon to look at paint colors and maybe find some ranch-themed decorations. He's got his heart set on horses and cattle and tractors—basically anything that reminds him of the ranch and the cowboy life he's so fascinated with."

"That boy has ranching in his blood. He gets that from your father's side of the family. Even you used to love helping with the cattle when you were his age, though you eventually decided teaching was your calling."

"Maybe Noah will stick with ranching," Eva said, then paused as she realized how natural it felt to think about her son's future in terms of this place, this community, and this way of life. "It would make Dad so happy to have someone in the family interested in carrying on the tradition."

They worked in comfortable silence for a few minutes. The rhythm of scraping and peeling created its own meditation, and Eva found her mind wandering to the conversation she'd been wanting to have with her mother since lunch at the Bluebird Café earlier in the week.

"Mom," she said finally, "at the café the other day, Lily and Pastor Sam mentioned that Cade has been going through some difficult times. They said something about a divorce and losing his ranch?"

Ruby's hands stilled on the scraper, and Eva could sense her mother's internal debate about how much information to share. After a moment, Ruby set down her tool and turned to face Eva with the expression of someone who'd made a decision to speak honestly.

"Oh, honey," Ruby said softly, her voice carrying the weight of genuine sadness. "It's been such a heartbreaking situation. I didn't want to burden you with someone else's troubles when you're dealing with such a big transition yourself. Your dad and I both decided not to mention it to you."

"I could tell something was wrong," Eva said, climbing down from the ladder. "The Cade I remember was so open and full of life, always ready with a smile or a joke. The man I saw when I came home barely seems like the same person."

Ruby's expression grew even more somber as she settled onto one of the plastic-covered chairs around the dining table. "His wife—ex-wife now—Rachel... she was a beautiful girl from Billings who seemed to love ranch life when they were dating. Cade was so happy when they got married, so sure he'd found someone who shared his dreams of building a life on his family's land."

Eva perched on the edge of the table, giving her mother her full attention as the story unfolded. "What happened?" she asked quietly, though part of her wasn't sure she wanted to know the details.

"Rachel started changing not too long after they got married... restless... just acting different," Ruby continued, her voice heavy with the sadness of someone who'd watched the tragedy unfold from the sidelines. "She wanted Cade to sell the ranch and move to the city. Said she was tired of the isolation and she wanted to be with her friends in the city. When he refused to give up his family's land, she started spending more and more time in Billings, claiming she needed the social interaction that ranch life couldn't provide."

"There was someone else?"

"A lawyer she met during one of her shopping trips," Ruby confirmed with a shake of her head. "The affair went on for months before Cade discovered it. And the worst part—the part that just destroyed him—was how calculated the whole thing was. This lawyer helped Rachel structure the divorce settlement to force the sale of the ranch. They knew exactly which assets to target to cause maximum financial damage."

The cruelty of it took Eva's breath away. "He lost his family's ranch because of the divorce?"

"Three generations of Mayer family history, gone in one devastating legal maneuver," Ruby said, her voice thick with emotion. "The ranch had some debt from improvements Cade had made—new equipment, upgraded facilities, things that would have paid for themselves in a few years. But the settlement required him to buy out Rachel's share of the property immediately, and there was no way to do that without selling everything. Between you and me... she came out of it all smelling like a rose and walked away proud as a peacock."

Eva felt tears pricking at her eyes as she imagined Cade's devastation. Losing a spouse was painful enough, but losing the land that represented his family's legacy, his identity, and his entire way of life—it was almost incomprehensible in its cruelty.

"That poor man," she whispered, understanding now why Cade seemed like a shadow of his former self. "How did he survive something like that?"

"Barely," Ruby said honestly. "After the divorce was finalized and he sold the ranch, the Cade you and I knew... he just disappeared. He'd take odd jobs here and there—construction work, temporary ranch hand positions—but he was so broken, so angry and hurt, that he couldn't seem to settle anywhere. People who tried to help him said it was like talking to a ghost of the person he used to be."

"How did he end up working for Dad?"

"Your daddy ran into him in town a little over eight months ago," Ruby explained, her expression softening with the memory. "Cade was picking up supplies for some temporary work he was doing, and Chuck said he looked terrible—thin, hollow-eyed, like he hadn't been sleeping or taking care of himself properly. They talked for a few minutes, and Chuck could see that Cade was drowning."

Eva could picture the scene perfectly—her kindhearted dad recognizing someone in need and immediately wanting to help, regardless of the personal complications it might create.

"So Dad offered him the foreman position?"

"Chuck came home that night and told me he'd hired Cade as our new foreman," Ruby said with a small smile. "Said he couldn't stand to see that boy wandering around lost when we had meaningful work and a decent place for him to live just sitting empty."

"That sounds exactly like Dad," Eva said, feeling a surge of pride for her father's generous spirit. "How has Cade been doing since then?"

Ruby considered the question carefully. "Better, in some ways. He's excellent at the job—knows ranching inside and out, works harder than any foreman we've ever had, and the ranch hands respect him completely. But personally... Eva, honey, that boy is still so hurt, so closed off from everyone and everything. He's polite and professional, but it's like he's built this fortress around his heart that no one can penetrate."

"He was always so full of dreams and hopes and life," Eva said softly, remembering the teenage Cade who'd talked enthusiastically about expanding his family's operation and raising children who would love the land as much as he did. "He had such big plans for the future, such faith that everything would work out if he just worked hard enough."

"That's the saddest part. Rachel destroyed his faith in love, in trust, and in the fundamental goodness of people. Cade used to be the kind of person who believed the best about everyone, who wore his heart on his sleeve, and who loved without reservation. Now he acts like he's afraid to care about anything or anyone."

Eva felt anger rising in her chest—not just at this Rachel's betrayal, but at the cosmic injustice of someone as good and loving as Cade being damaged so severely by someone he'd trusted completely. The teenage boy she'd loved had possessed such a generous heart, such an instinctive understanding of loyalty and commitment. To think that someone had taken those beautiful qualities and used them as weapons against him made her want to find Rachel and give her a piece of her mind.

"It's affected his relationship with God. Cade used to have such strong faith. Now your daddy says he declines each of his invitations to church, claims he's too busy, or just makes some other excuse. I think he feels like God abandoned him when everything fell apart."

The complete picture of Cade's devastation was almost too much to bear. Eva had experienced her own crisis of faith after David's sudden death and had struggled with questions about divine justice and the fairness of losing someone so young and good. But she'd ultimately found comfort in the belief that David's love was a gift she'd been blessed to receive, even if only briefly.

"We love that boy like he's our son," Ruby said, her voice breaking slightly with emotion. "When you two were dating in high school, Chuck and I used to joke that we'd already gained a son-in-law, even if it would be a few years before it became official. Cade was always respectful, hardworking, and so obviously devoted to you that we never worried about your safety or happiness when you were with him."

Eva felt her eyes filling with tears again as she remembered how easily Cade had fit into their family dynamic—helping with ranch work without being asked, charming her mother with his politeness and humor, and earning her father's respect through his genuine interest in learning and his natural affinity for ranch work.

"Even after you two broke up, and you went to college, we kept hoping he'd find someone who deserved him," Ruby continued. "When he married Rachel, we were so happy for him, so sure he'd found his person. And when it all fell apart... honey, it broke our hearts almost as much as it broke his."

"I can't believe someone could be so cruel," Eva said, wiping away a tear that had escaped despite her efforts to maintain composure. "To systematically destroy someone's life like that, to take advantage of their love and use it as a weapon—it's unforgivable."

"Which is why," Ruby said gently, reaching over to take Eva's hand, "I think it might be good for Cade to have you back in his life. Not in a romantic way—I know that would be complicated for everyone involved—but as a friend. Someone who knew him when he was whole, who can remind him that he's still the same good man underneath all that pain and anger."

Eva looked at her mother in surprise. "You think I should reach out to him?"

"I think," Ruby said carefully, "that Cade needs to remember there are still good people in the world. People who can be trusted and who keep their word. You represent his past, Eva—a time when he was happy and hopeful. Maybe your friendship and loving and kind spirit could help him find his way back to that person."

The suggestion both thrilled and terrified Eva. Part of her desperately wanted to help Cade, to find some way to ease the pain she could see lurking. But another part recognized the dangers inherent in getting too involved with someone who still held a piece of her heart.

"I don't know if I'm the right person for that," Eva said honestly. "Our history... and I have Noah to think about. I can't risk him getting attached to someone who might not be emotionally available."

"I'm not suggesting you solve all of Cade's problems," Ruby clarified. "Just that you be kind to him. Include him when it feels natural, and let him know he's welcome, without pressuring him to open up before he's ready. Sometimes people need to be reminded that they're not alone in the world."

As Eva thought about this, Ruby walked toward the kitchen, interrupting their conversation. "Let me just rinse this adhesive off my hands," Ruby called over her shoulder. "This chemical residue is going to permanently attach my fingers if I don't—"

Her words were cut off by a sharp yelp, followed immediately by the unmistakable sound of water gushing with considerable force. Eva jumped up from her perch and rushed toward the kitchen to find her mother standing in the center of what was rapidly becoming a small indoor pool.

"The pipe under the sink!" Ruby yelled, gesturing helplessly at the cabinet that was producing an impressive fountain of water. "I barely touched the faucet and—"

Eva didn't wait to hear the rest of the explanation. She lunged across the slippery floor, her sock-clad feet sliding comically as she attempted to navigate the growing puddle. Dropping to her knees in front of the sink cabinet, she yanked open the doors and crawled halfway inside the narrow space, feeling around blindly for the shutoff valve while water continued to spray in every direction.

"Where is it?" she called out, her voice muffled by the cabinet walls as water soaked through her shirt and dripped from her hair. "There has to be a shutoff valve somewhere under here!"

Eva finally located what felt like a valve handle partially hidden behind the main pipe. She twisted it counterclockwise with all her strength, praying she was turning it in the right direction and not making the situation worse. After what felt like an eternity, the rushing water began to slow, then stopped completely.

"Got it!" Eva announced triumphantly, then attempted to back out of the cabinet. Her shirt was soaked, her hair was dripping, and she was pretty sure she had dusty cabinet grime smudged across her face.

Ruby stood in the middle of the kitchen, looking equally bedraggled, her clothes wet and her hair escaping its clip in damp tendrils. For a moment, they simply stared at each other, taking in the sight of their waterlogged appearance and the small pond that now covered most of the kitchen floor.

Then Ruby began to laugh—not just a chuckle, but the kind of full-body, shoulder-shaking laughter that was impossible to resist. Eva joined in, and soon they were both giggling like schoolgirls at the absurdity of their situation.

"Well," Eva gasped between fits of laughter, "I guess we can add plumbing disasters to the list of renovation adventures."

"At least it happened while we were both here to deal with it," Ruby said, attempting to wring water out of her shirt with limited success. "Can you imagine if this had happened in the middle of the night with guests staying upstairs?"

Eva grabbed a handful of kitchen towels and began attempting to mop up the worst of the flooding, though it was clearly going to require more serious intervention to properly dry the floor and assess any damage.

"I'll call your daddy," Ruby said, fishing her cell phone out of her back pocket. "He'll need to bring some tools and see if this is something he can fix, or if we need to call a plumber."

Eva nodded, still dripping and grinning as she surveyed the chaos that had happened in less than five minutes. The dining room looked like a wallpaper removal explosion; the kitchen resembled the aftermath of a small flood, and both she and her mother looked like they'd been through a car wash without the benefit of a car.

"You know what?" Eva said, suddenly struck by the ridiculousness of their situation. "This is exactly the kind of disaster that Aunt Connie would have handled with grace and humor. She'd probably have guests helping with the cleanup and turning it into an adventure they'd remember forever."

"That's the spirit," Ruby agreed. "Every old house comes with its share of surprises. The trick is learning to roll with them instead of letting them derail you."

Chapter 11

Noah's excited chatter filled the cab of the truck, punctuated by Chuck's patient responses and the occasional laugh that spoke of a grandfather thoroughly enjoying his time with an enthusiastic eight-year-old grandson.

"And then WHOOSH! Water went everywhere! It was like a fountain! And I got to hold the big wrench, and it was really heavy, and the water stopped, and Grandpa said I was a good helper!" Noah said as they climbed out of the truck.

"You did good work today, partner," Chuck said, ruffling Noah's hair with casual affection. "Having an extra pair of hands made that job go twice as fast today."

Cade followed them toward the front door of Eva's home.

"Mom's gonna want to hear everything," Noah continued as he hopped up the porch steps.

The front door opened, revealing Ruby with a look of relief on her face. Behind her, Eva appeared. She looked as if she'd been wrestling with some kind of home improvement project—her hair was escaping its ponytail in wet, wispy tendrils, and there were smudges of dirt on her cheek.

"Thank goodness you're here," Ruby said, stepping aside to let them enter. "We've had a little incident."

"More like a disaster," Eva added with a rueful laugh, gesturing toward the kitchen. "The pipe under the sink decided to give up the ghost right in the middle of our wallpaper removal project."

"Let's check it out," Chuck said, already heading toward the kitchen with the purposeful stride of a man who'd dealt with his share of plumbing emergencies over the years.

Cade followed, trying not to notice the way Eva's jeans hugged her curves or how the afternoon light streaming through the kitchen windows brought out the copper highlights in her hair. He was here to help with a plumbing problem, nothing more, and the sooner he could focus on pipes and fittings, the better.

"I was trying to rinse the adhesive remover off my hands," Ruby explained. "I barely turned the faucet handle, and suddenly water was shooting everywhere. It was shooting from the faucet and from the pipes in the cabinet."

Noah immediately positioned himself next to Cade, clearly considering himself part of the repair crew. "Can I help fix it?" he asked eagerly. "I'm really good at holding tools and stuff."

"Let's see what needs doing first," Chuck said, crouching down to examine the cabinet under the sink. "Cade here is a wizard with plumbing repairs. Saved us a fortune in plumbing bills over the years."

Cade felt heat rise in his cheeks at the praise, uncomfortable with being singled out for skills that seemed perfectly ordinary to him. "Most ranchers learn to handle simple repairs out of necessity," he said quietly, joining Chuck and Noah in front of the open cabinet.

But as he examined the burst pipe and traced the connections with the practiced eye of someone who'd spent years maintaining water systems on his own ranch, Cade could see this wasn't going to be a simple fix. The pipes were old—probably original to the house's construction.

"Grab that flashlight," he said to Noah, who immediately scrambled to grab the requested tool off the counter and proudly assumed the position of official light-holder. The beam illuminated the full extent of the damage.

"What's the verdict?" Eva asked, crouching down beside them with genuine concern in her voice. Her proximity sent an unwelcome rush of awareness through Cade—the scent of her shampoo and the warmth of her body close enough to feel.

"The pipe cracked right at this joint," Cade explained, pointing to the obvious failure point while trying to ignore the way Eva leaned closer to see what he was indicating. "But the problem is that all these supply lines are old enough that they're probably near the end of their useful life. Fixing just this one section might buy you some time, but you'd be looking at similar failures down the road."

Chuck nodded grimly, his assessment clearly reaching the same conclusion. "Better to replace the whole run instead of just putting a band aid in place. Do it right the first time."

"And the faucet?" Eva asked, gesturing toward the fixture that had apparently cracked during the morning's excitement.

Cade straightened up to examine the faucet more closely, noting the hairline fracture that ran along the base of the spout. "That'll need replacing, too. Looks like the pressure surge when the pipe burst was more than the old fixture could handle."

"Can you hold the flashlight a little higher?" he asked Noah, who immediately adjusted his position with the serious concentration of someone taking his job very seriously. "Perfect. You're getting good at this."

The praise brought a gigantic grin to Noah's face.

"We should probably check the basement too," Chuck suggested.

"Good thinking," Cade agreed.

The basement inspection became a family affair, with Ruby and Eva joining the expedition along with Noah. The basement of the old Victorian house was exactly what Cade had expected—stone foundation walls, wooden floor joists, and an array of pipes and electrical systems.

"Most of this looks pretty solid," Chuck observed, running his hands along the main water line that fed the kitchen. "No leaks or corrosion."

Cade worked his way along the supply lines, testing connections and checking for signs of wear or deterioration. The basement was cool and slightly damp, with that musty scent that seemed inherent to old houses. The cramped space in one corner required him to work in close proximity to Eva as she held a flashlight to illuminate the area.

"This shutoff valve is completely seized," he said. The valve wheel wouldn't budge despite his considerable effort, and the corrosion around the threads suggested it had been stuck for quite some time.

"Not good," Eva said, moving closer to see what he'd found. Her shoulder brushed against his arm as she positioned herself to get a better view, and Cade had to concentrate harder than should have been necessary on the technical aspects of the plumbing system.

"If you ever need to shut off water to the kitchen completely in an emergency, you can't do it from here," he explained, stepping back slightly to create more space between them. "You'd have to shut off the main line to the whole house, which isn't ideal if you're running a bed and breakfast."

"So it needs to be replaced."

"I'd recommend it," Cade said, testing another connection further down the line. "While we're doing the kitchen work anyway, it makes sense to upgrade anything that might cause problems later."

As they made their way back upstairs, Cade was impressed by Eva's calm approach to the repairs. Rather than becoming overwhelmed by the scope of work required, she seemed as if repairs were expected and was calm, with no unnecessary drama.

"So, let's make a shopping list," Chuck said once they'd reassembled in the kitchen, pulling out a small notebook from his shirt pocket.

Cade considered the full scope of repairs they'd identified, mentally cataloging the parts and materials they'd need to complete the job properly. "Supply lines for under the sink, a new faucet assembly, two shutoff valves, and probably some additional fittings, depending on how the connections work out."

"Pipe dope, plumber's tape, sandpaper for the joints… might as well get everything and start a supply stash for Eva," Chuck added.

"I can run into town and pick everything up," Eva interjected. "Just give me a detailed list, and Noah and I will make an adventure out of it."

"No need to trouble yourself," Cade said automatically, his instinct to handle problems independently kicking in. "I can run up to Morrison's Hardware and be back within an hour."

"Actually, why don't you both go together? That way, Eva can pick out the faucet she wants, and you, Cade, can get everything needed without Eva questioning if she's buying the right things," Ruby said.

The suggestion hit Cade right in the chest, perfectly logical and completely reasonable while simultaneously creating exactly the kind of interaction with Eva he'd been wanting to avoid.

"That's actually a great idea," Eva said, smiling at her mom's suggestion. "I should learn more about this stuff anyway."

"Chuck and I will take Noah back to the ranch and get a dinner started. You two can join us when you finish shopping. I think I'll just pull a couple of pizzas out of the freezer," Ruby said with the satisfied smile of someone whose plan was coming together perfectly.

Cade felt like he was being swept along by forces beyond his control. Noah was already agreeing enthusiastically to the plan, clearly excited about the prospect of more time at the ranch and pizza for dinner, while Chuck nodded approvingly at his wife's suggestion.

"I really don't mind going alone," Cade tried one more time.

"Nope," Eva said firmly. "Give me fifteen minutes to change out of these wet clothes and try to make my hair look like something other than a bird's nest, and then we'll head into town together."

She reached out and gave his arm a playful nudge, the casual contact sending a jolt of warmth through his system. "Don't you dare try to sneak off without me, Cade Mayer. I need to learn this stuff, and you're my appointed teacher."

With that declaration, she headed toward the stairs with the determined stride of someone who'd made up her mind and wasn't interested in hearing objections. Cade watched her go and realized that he was about to face a big test in his choice to keep a safe distance.

"Well," Chuck said with barely concealed amusement as he patted Cade on the shoulder, "looks like you've got your afternoon planned out for you. Take good care of my girl."

Ruby was already ushering Noah toward the front door. "Come on, sweetheart, let's get you back to the ranch and see if we can find some of those cookies I made yesterday."

"Can I help Grandpa with more chores?" Noah asked.

"If you're not too tired from all that fence work this morning... sure, why not!" Chuck said with a grin as he followed his wife and grandson out the front door.

Cade stood alone in the kitchen, feeling like he'd just been swept up into a tornado.

Chapter 12

Cade sat on the front porch steps of the bed and breakfast, his hands clasped loosely between his knees, as he stared out at the mountain vista that never failed to calm him. The afternoon sun was warm, and the distant sound of cattle lowing provided a soundtrack that usually brought him comfort. His mind, however, was too occupied with the prospect of spending the next hour alone with Eva to find much peace in the familiar surroundings.

The screen door opened behind him with a soft creak, followed by the sound of Eva's footsteps as she emerged from the house. He turned to look over his shoulder and felt his breath catch slightly at the sight of her. She'd changed into comfortable clothes—soft gray yoga pants that hugged her legs, a loose-fitting pink t-shirt that somehow managed to be both casual and feminine, and bright pink tennis shoes. Her hair was pulled back in a simple ponytail that emphasized the graceful line of her neck.

She looked young and fresh and completely unaware of the effect she was having on him.

"You look like you're lost in some pretty deep thoughts," Eva said with a laugh, closing the door behind her and slinging a small purse over her shoulder. "Planning your escape route?"

The teasing note in her voice reminded him so strongly of the girl she'd been in high school—playful and confident and utterly comfortable in her own skin—that for a moment he forgot all the reasons why this shopping trip was a terrible idea. Then reality reasserted itself, and he stood up.

"Just thinking about the parts list."

Eva's smile suggested she didn't entirely believe his explanation, but she didn't challenge him on it. Instead, she gestured toward his red pickup truck parked in the driveway. "Ready to educate me about the mysteries of plumbing supplies?"

Cade nodded and headed toward the truck. When they reached the passenger side, he automatically moved to open the door for her—a habit his mother had drilled into him so thoroughly that it was second nature.

"Thank you. I'd forgotten how nice it is to have a man open a door for me."

He closed her door without responding and walked around to the driver's side, using the few extra seconds to compose himself before settling behind the wheel.

He started the truck and drove around the circular driveway, turning onto the main road. Eva adjusted the air conditioning vents and fiddled with the radio until she found a country station playing something soft and melodic.

"I can't believe how much this valley has grown since I moved away," Eva said as they headed toward town, her voice bright with the kind of enthusiasm that seemed to come naturally to her. "There are at least three new houses on this road alone, and Mom said they're talking about expanding the school district to accommodate all the families moving in from the cities."

Cade made a noncommittal sound of agreement, keeping his eyes focused on the road while Eva continued her observation of the changes that had occurred during her years away. Her voice was pleasant and familiar, washing over him like a comfortable blanket.

"And tourism seems to be picking up too," she continued, apparently unfazed by his lack of verbal participation in the conversation. "I saw four RVs with out-of-state plates just the other day when I was in town picking up groceries. That's got to be good for local businesses."

"Mm-hmm," Cade responded.

"Oh, and I meant to tell you—Noah hasn't stopped talking about helping you on the ranch," Eva said, turning slightly in her seat so she could see his profile while she talked. "He's absolutely convinced that he knows what he wants to do when he's older."

"He's a good kid."

"You're good with him. He needs that kind of steady male influence in his life. It means more to me than you probably realize... I appreciate your patience with him."

The conversation was veering into territory that felt too personal, too loaded with implications that Cade couldn't afford to explore. He focused on navigating the streets of downtown Riverbend Valley.

"Morrison's Hardware," he said a few moments later, pointing toward the red brick building that had been serving the hardware needs of Riverbend Valley for over forty years. "Old Jim Morrison still runs it, but his son has been helping him out more and more lately."

Eva peered through the windshield at the store's vintage sign and well-maintained exterior. "It looks exactly the same as it did when I was in high school."

Cade pulled into a parking space near the front entrance and turned off the engine, then sat for a moment with his hands still gripping the steering wheel. The silence in the cab suddenly felt charged with possibility and danger in equal measure, and he realized that Eva had stopped her cheerful chatter.

"You know," he said finally, turning to meet her gaze directly for the first time since they'd gotten in the truck, "you're doing that thing you used to do when you were nervous."

Eva's eyebrows rose in question. "What thing?"

"Talking a mile a minute about everything except what's actually on your mind," Cade said, and was surprised to hear a note of gentle teasing in his own voice. "You did it before our first date, and before you had to give that speech for student council, and pretty much any time you were trying not to think too hard about something that was making you anxious."

Cade immediately regretted saying it. It was too personal, too much of an acknowledgment that he remembered details about her personality and habits that he had no business remembering. But Eva's face lit up with a laugh that was completely genuine and thoroughly delighted.

"I can't believe you remember that," she said, shaking her head with apparent amazement. "I thought I was being so smooth and casual."

"You were many things," Cade said, climbing out of the truck, "but smooth and casual when you were nervous was never one of them."

He walked around to open her door. Eva stepped down from the truck with a grace that made him acutely aware of her proximity, and the scent of her perfume threatened to derail his composure entirely.

"Well," Eva said as they headed toward the hardware store entrance, "I guess some things never change."

"Morning, Cade," Jake Morrison called out from behind the main counter, looking up from the inventory list he'd been checking as they entered the store. At thirty, Jake had inherited both his father's business acumen and his friendly demeanor, making him popular with everyone from weekend DIY enthusiasts to professional contractors. "What brings you in today?"

"Plumbing emergency at the Connie Turner's place," Cade replied as he guided Eva toward the aisle that housed pipes, fittings, and related supplies. "Need to replace some old supply lines and a kitchen faucet."

"Ah, the old Turner bed and breakfast," Jake said with a knowing nod. "Heard you're opening it back up, Eva. That's exciting news for the valley. Welcome back."

Eva smiled and offered a small wave. "Just moved back home a few days ago, and I'm already discovering all the joys of owning a century-old house."

"Well, you're in good hands with Cade," Jake said with obvious respect. "He knows his way around plumbing better than most."

The praise made Cade uncomfortable, as it always did, but he accepted it with a brief nod and continued toward the plumbing supplies. Eva followed, her curiosity evident as she took in the bewildering array of pipes, joints, and fittings that lined the shelves from floor to ceiling.

"Okay," she said, stopping in front of a display that featured dozens of different types of connectors. "This is where you're going to have to explain things like I'm five years old. I can change a light bulb, unclog a toilet, and turn off a water valve, but beyond that, plumbing might as well be rocket science."

Cade grinned at her frank admission of inexperience.

"It's not as complicated as it looks," he said, reaching for a package of supply lines and showing them to her. "These are what we'll use to replace the old pipes under your sink. They're more durable than the original pipes and less likely to crack under pressure."

Eva examined the package with the focused attention of someone genuinely interested in learning. "And these connect to the faucet how?"

Cade selected the appropriate fittings and demonstrated how the connections would work, explaining the basic principles of water pressure and pipe sizing in terms that were technical enough to be accurate but simple enough for a beginner to understand. Eva asked intelligent questions and seemed to grasp the concepts quickly, confirming his impression that her mind was as sharp as he remembered.

"Now for the shutoff valves," he continued, moving to another section of the aisle and locating the replacement parts they'd need. "This one has a quarter-turn handle instead of the old wheel-style valve that's seized up down in your basement. Much easier to operate in an emergency."

"Makes sense," Eva said, taking the valve from him and examining its construction with obvious interest. "And all of this connects together with those fitting things you showed me?"

"Yep. Just like putting a puzzle together," Cade confirmed, gathering the additional supplies they'd need—pipe dope, plumber's tape, and the miscellaneous fittings that always seemed necessary once you actually started taking pipes apart.

As they worked their way through the supply list, Cade relaxed a bit as he explained things. Eva's questions were thoughtful and practical, and her obvious appreciation for his knowledge was gratifying in ways he hadn't expected.

"Now comes the fun part," Eva said as they finished gathering the pipe-related supplies. "Picking out a new faucet that won't look completely out of place on a cast iron kitchen sink."

The faucet display occupied an entire wall of the store, featuring everything from ultra-modern stainless-steel designs to reproduction antique fixtures that would have been appropriate for Aunt Connie's era. Eva studied the options with the same focused attention she'd given to the plumbing supplies, but Cade could see that the aesthetic choices were more challenging for her than the technical aspects had been.

"What do you think?" she asked, gesturing toward a brass fixture with ceramic handles that struck a balance between period authenticity and modern functionality. "Too fancy for a working kitchen?"

Cade examined the faucet she'd indicated, testing the weight and build quality. "It's well made," he said, "and the style fits the house. More importantly, it's got ceramic cartridges instead of rubber washers, so it's less likely to develop leaks down the road."

"Practical and pretty," Eva said with obvious satisfaction. "I like a man who appreciates both form and function."

The comment was innocent enough, but something about the way she said it—or maybe the way she looked at him while she said it—made him feel as if a bull had rammed his chest. For a moment, he remembered what it felt like to be the kind of man Eva Turner looked at with approval and genuine affection.

"Let me grab one more thing," he said, turning away before his expression could reveal too much of what he was thinking. "You'll want new supply lines for the faucet connections too, just to be safe."

As he selected the additional parts, Cade became aware that they'd attracted some attention from other customers in the store. Riverbend Valley was small enough that everyone knew everyone, and his presence with Eva—especially given their shared history—was bound to generate some interest and probably a fair amount of speculation.

"Cade! Eva Turner!" The voice belonged to Helen Morrison, Jake's mother, and the unofficial social coordinator for half the valley. She approached with the determined stride of someone who'd spotted an opportunity for catching up on the latest community gossip. "I heard you were back in town, dear. How wonderful! And aren't you more gorgeous than when you left!"

"It's Eva Blankenship now, Mrs. Morrison," Eva corrected gently, "and it's good to see you. I was just learning about plumbing supplies from Cade here."

Helen's eyes sparkled with the kind of interest that suggested she was already composing the story she'd share with her bridge club later that week. "How nice that you two are working together again. Just like old times."

Cade's jaw tightened, but Eva handled the comment with gracious humor. "Cade's been kind enough to help with some repairs at the bed and breakfast. I'm discovering that old houses require a lot more maintenance knowledge than I currently have."

"Well, you couldn't ask for a better teacher," Helen said with obvious approval. "Cade's helped half the families in this valley with one project or another over the years. We're all so grateful to have him."

The conversation continued for a few more minutes, with Helen asking about Eva's plans for the bed and breakfast and sharing updates about various community members Eva remembered from her youth. Cade listened with half his attention, while the other half focused on the way Eva handled the social interaction—warm and interested without being overly familiar, polite without encouraging excessive curiosity about her personal life.

When Helen finally excused herself, Eva turned to Cade with a rueful smile. "By dinner time, half the valley will know we went shopping together."

"Does that bother you?" Cade asked, genuinely curious.

"No. People are going to talk, regardless. Might as well give them something harmless to speculate about instead of letting them make up more interesting stories."

Her practical attitude surprised him and impressed him in equal measure. The Eva he remembered from high school had been more concerned with what people thought and more careful about maintaining the right kind of reputation. This version seemed more confident in her own skin and more willing to let others draw their own conclusions without feeling the need to manage their opinions.

At the checkout counter, the total came to more than Cade had expected, but Eva handed over her debit card without hesitation. It was another reminder that her life had taken a very different path from his own—she had resources and options that his recent circumstances had eliminated, a stability that he was still working to rebuild piece by piece.

As they made their way back to his truck, his mind swirled with thoughts. Eva was a woman who owned property and had the resources to maintain her lifestyle while starting her own business, and he was an employee living in someone else's cabin and starting over from scratch at thirty years old.

The drive back to the bed and breakfast passed more quietly than the trip into town, with Eva seeming content to look out the window at the passing scenery instead of maintaining her earlier stream of conversation. Cade found the silence almost as dangerous as her chatter had been—it felt too natural, too much like easy companionship.

When he pulled up and parked in front of her parents' home, she looked at him and said, "That wasn't nearly as painful as you were expecting, was it?"

"What makes you think I was expecting it to be painful?"

"Oh, just the way you looked like you were being led to the gallows when Mom suggested we go together," Eva said with a laugh. "And the fact that you've been treating me like I might explode if you say the wrong thing."

Eva opened the passenger door and stepped down, turning back to look at him.

"For what it's worth," she said, "I had a nice time today. It felt good spending time with someone who remembers who I used to be, even if we're both very different people now."

The honesty in her voice stripped away his defenses more effectively than any argument or persuasion could have done. For a moment, Cade found himself looking at her not as a complication to be avoided or a temptation to be resisted, but simply as Eva—the woman who'd been his first love and was now trying to build a new life for herself in the place where they'd both grown up.

"Try not to smile," Eva said with a grin that was pure mischief. "Your face might crack from the unfamiliar exercise."

Despite himself, Cade felt the corners of his mouth lifting in what was dangerously close to a real smile. The realization that she'd noticed his struggle to maintain his serious demeanor was both embarrassing and oddly liberating—apparently his poker face needed more work.

"Come on," Eva continued. "Let's go have some pizza."

Cade shook his head as she shut the door and walked toward the house.

Chapter 13

The aroma of melted cheese and pizza sauce filled the Turner family dining room as Eva reached for another slice, savoring both the food and the warm conversation flowing around the table. Noah sat between his grandparents, regaling them with detailed accounts of his childhood adventures, while Chuck nodded with grandfatherly approval and Ruby refilled everyone's glasses with sweet tea.

Cade occupied the chair across from Eva, working through his second piece of pizza with the same careful, quiet attention he brought to everything else. Eva caught herself studying the way the evening light from the kitchen window caught the silver threads at his temples, remembering when his hair had been uniformly dark and he'd worn it longer, constantly falling into his eyes when they were younger.

"And then Cade showed me how the post puller works," Noah continued enthusiastically, gesturing with a pizza crust that dripped sauce onto his napkin. "It's magic. He said I was good at it too, didn't you, Cade?"

"You caught on fast," Cade confirmed.

"Speaking of catching on to things," Eva said, seizing the opening to draw Cade into more conversation, "do you remember that time during our junior year when you tried to teach me to back a horse trailer and I nearly took out Dad's fence post?"

Chuck's laughter boomed across the table. "I remember that! I came running from the barn thinking we were under attack from the sound of all that commotion."

Ruby's eyes sparkled with maternal mischief. "You were so patient, Cade, standing there giving directions while Eva kept turning the wheel the wrong way and getting more frustrated by the minute."

"I was not getting frustrated," Eva protested with mock indignation, though her smile gave away the truth. "I was demonstrating my natural leadership abilities by offering creative suggestions about the trailer's questionable engineering."

"Is that what you're calling it?" Cade asked, and Eva felt her heart skip at the hint of teasing in his voice. "Because I remember you informing the trailer that it was being deliberately uncooperative and needed an attitude adjustment."

Noah giggled. "Mom still talks to things that don't work right. She talked to our dishwasher in Bozeman all the time."

"That dishwasher had it coming," Eva said with dignity, pleased to see Cade's mouth quirk upward. "And for the record, I eventually mastered the art of trailer backing. It just took some practice and a few more fence posts."

"A few more?" Chuck shook his head with amused exasperation. "Eva, honey, you managed to clip nine different posts before you figured out which direction to turn that wheel."

"But she got it in the end," Ruby said. "And she never gave up, which is what mattered most."

"What about the time you decided to help with moving our cattle to the south pasture?" Eva continued, directing her attention to Cade with a grin that dared him to deny the memory. "You were so determined to impress my dad with your herding skills."

Cade's expression grew wary, but there was a hint of amusement lurking in his green eyes. "I recall that particular adventure differently than you probably do."

"Oh, this should be good," Chuck said, settling back in his chair with obvious anticipation. "I don't think I ever heard the full story of what happened that day."

"Well," Eva began with theatrical seriousness, "Cade had been studying cattle handling techniques from some library book—"

"It was a legitimate agricultural manual," Cade interjected mildly.

"—and he was absolutely convinced that he could move those cattle more efficiently than we'd been doing it for generations," Eva continued, ignoring his protest. "He had this whole scientific approach mapped out about optimal spacing and movement patterns."

Noah bounced in his seat. "What happened?"

"Let's just say that cattle don't actually read agricultural manuals," Cade said dryly.

"The lead steer took one look at Cade's 'scientifically optimal positioning' and decided to head in completely the opposite direction," Eva explained to Noah. "Which caused a domino effect that scattered the entire herd across three different pastures."

Ruby laughed so hard she had to dab her eyes with her napkin. "I remember that day! Your daddy came in for lunch looking like he'd been through a hurricane, and Cade looked like he wanted to disappear into the ground."

"It took us four hours to round them all up again," Chuck added with good-natured humor. "But I'll give you credit, Cade—you worked harder than anyone to fix what went wrong, and you never tried to make excuses."

"I learned a valuable lesson about the difference between theory and practice," Cade said, and Eva was delighted to hear genuine humor creeping into his voice. "And about respecting the wisdom of people who've been doing something successfully for decades."

"You also learned to listen to your girlfriend when she tried to warn you that the lead steer was a troublemaker," Eva added with satisfaction.

"You did try to warn me," Cade admitted, meeting her eyes for a moment longer than was strictly necessary. "I was just too stubborn to listen."

The acknowledgment carried more weight than a simple admission about teenage cattle-herding mishaps. Eva felt her pulse quicken at the intensity in his gaze.

"Oh, that reminds me of the time you tried to fix the barn door latch with nothing but determination and a roll of duct tape," Ruby said to Cade. "Chuck found you out there with that contraption you'd rigged up, muttering under your breath about 'temporary solutions becoming permanent fixtures.'"

"That latch held for another year," Cade protested with what sounded suspiciously like pride.

"It also looked like something a mad scientist would build," Chuck pointed out. "But I have to admit, it was effective."

Noah was following this exchange with fascination, clearly enchanted by these glimpses into the adults' shared history. "Tell me another story," he demanded. "About when you and Mom were in school together."

Eva grinned, "Hmm mmm, let me think on this, Noah."

But Cade surprised her by volunteering a story of his own.

"Your mom once convinced me to enter the county fair's pie-eating contest," he said. "She'd been practicing her baking skills for weeks, determined to perfect her apple pie recipe for the baking competition."

"I remember that!" Ruby exclaimed. "Eva, you were so worried about getting the spices just right."

"I must have made a dozen practice pies," Eva agreed, remembering the intensive preparation that had taken over the kitchen for weeks. "And Cade volunteered to be my official taste-tester, which meant he'd already eaten enough pie to feed a small army before the actual contest."

"But you insisted that I needed to enter the pie-eating competition 'just for fun,'" Cade continued. "Even though I was already so sick of pie that the thought of eating another bite made me queasy."

Noah's eyes went wide. "Did you win?"

"He came in dead last," Eva said with affectionate remembrance. "He managed to eat exactly half a pie before he turned green and had to excuse himself from the competition."

"But your pie won first place in the baking contest," Cade added, looking directly at Eva. "Which was all that really mattered."

"You were such a good sport about it," Eva said. "Even when Mrs. Henderson's grandson won the contest by eating seven whole pies."

"Seven pies? Really?" Noah asked in amazement.

"Some mysteries of the universe are beyond our understanding," Chuck said solemnly.

The conversation continued to flow naturally around the table, with each story leading to another and laughter punctuating the easy exchange of memories. Eva watched Cade's gradual transformation throughout the meal—his shoulders relaxing, his responses becoming more natural, and occasional glimpses of genuine humor.

This was the man she remembered, she realized with a pang of longing. Underneath all the pain and defensiveness, he was still the same person who'd been willing to make a fool of himself at a county fair because it mattered to someone he cared about.

"So, what are we going to do tomorrow?" Noah asked suddenly, his voice bright with anticipation as he finished the last bite of his pizza. "Can we ride horses? Can I rope something? Do more fence stuff?"

"Well, sweetheart, before we can do any of those things, we need to get the water pipes fixed at our house. That has to be the priority."

"We should probably head back now and get started on those repairs," Cade said.

"Now hold on just a minute," Chuck interrupted with paternal authority, raising his hand to stop Cade. "We've all had enough work for one day. I think it's time we grabbed one of Noah's games and had ourselves some fun this evening."

Eva felt a rush of affection for her father's timing. "That's a wonderful idea, Dad."

Ruby clapped her hands together with enthusiasm. "Perfect! We all need to take a break from work sometimes and just enjoy being together."

But Cade was already shaking his head. "I'll let you all enjoy the rest of your evening—"

"Now, Cade," Ruby said with the gentle firmness, "Don't you leave... stay and have some fun with us."

Cade looked across the table at Eva with a questioning expression.

"Family game night," she said firmly. "It's settled, and you're playing."

Before Cade could formulate another protest, Noah had already scrambled down from his chair. "I'll get the game!" he announced, racing toward the living room where the games were stored.

"Cade, you and I and Noah can attack those water pipes first thing in the mornin'. The ranch hands can handle everything here on the ranch while we get Eva's water situation sorted out," Chuck said.

Cade looked like he was still searching for a graceful way to excuse himself, but Noah's return cut off any further discussion. The boy came running back into the dining room with a colorful box clutched triumphantly in his hands.

"Chutes and Ladders!" Noah announced with the pride of someone presenting a priceless treasure.

"I haven't played that game in months," Eva said with genuine delight, clearing space on the table as Ruby began gathering the empty pizza plates.

Ruby returned from the kitchen with a plate of her homemade chocolate chip cookies. "Can't have proper family game night without cookies," she declared.

Eva watched Cade's face as he took in the scene unfolding around him—the bright game board, Noah's excited explanations of the rules, and her parents' comfortable inclusion of him. She could see the internal battle playing out in his expression.

"Cade, you can be the red piece. Red's a good color for cowboys, and it's a lucky color." Noah said.

After a moment's hesitation, he accepted the red game piece Noah handed him.

"Youngest player goes first," Ruby announced, which meant Noah got to take the inaugural spin. The spinner clicked merrily around its circle before landing on six, and Noah moved his blue piece with obvious satisfaction.

"Good start," Eva said encouragingly, taking her turn and landing on a space that immediately sent her sliding down a chute. "Well, that didn't last long."

"That's the beauty of this game," Chuck said as he spun a three and moved his green piece accordingly. "Just when you think you've got momentum, life throws you a curve."

When Cade's turn came, he spun the dial, landing on a five that placed him on a ladder square. As his red piece climbed several levels, Noah cheered as if Cade had just accomplished something genuinely heroic.

"See? Red's a lucky color... that's why I gave it to you!" Noah exclaimed.

Cade's smile was completely unguarded—brief, but real enough to make Eva's heart skip a beat.

The game continued, punctuated by Noah's running commentary, Chuck's strategic observations, and Ruby's cheerful encouragement of everyone's moves. Eva found herself watching Cade more than the game board, noting the gradual relaxation in his posture as the evening progressed and the way his responses became more natural and less guarded.

When Noah landed on the longest ladder in the game and shot from square fifteen to square ninety-three, his whoop of triumph was exuberant.

"I might win!" Noah announced, doing a little victory dance in his chair.

"Don't count your chickens before they hatch," Eva warned, though she was grinning at her son's enthusiasm.

"Besides," Cade added, "sometimes the journey is more important than getting to the finish line first."

"Wise words from a wise man," Ruby said.

The game continued for another twenty minutes, with the lead changing hands multiple times as players encountered both helpful ladders and treacherous chutes. Noah's early advantage was gradually eroded by a series of unfortunate spins, while Eva made steady progress through moderate luck.

But it was Cade who ultimately won, his red piece climbing the final ladder to square one hundred amid Noah's enthusiastic applause and the adults' good-natured congratulations.

"Beginner's luck," Cade said modestly.

"Skill and strategy," Chuck corrected.

"Can we play again?" Noah asked hopefully, already gathering the game pieces for another round.

"It's bedtime for certain young men," Eva said gently.

"Aw, Mom..."

"How about we save another game for tomorrow?" Ruby suggested.

"Promise?"

"Cross my heart," Ruby said solemnly, making the appropriate gesture.

"Cade, will you play games tomorrow, too?" Noah asked.

Eva held her breath, watching Cade's face as he processed Noah's innocent request.

"We'll see how the day goes," Cade said.

Noah seemed satisfied with this non-answer, apparently interpreting Cade's words more optimistically than they'd probably been intended. "Okay! I'm gonna help with the pipes, so we'll get done faster."

As the family began the process of cleaning up after their evening's entertainment, Eva watched Cade's interactions with each member of her family. He helped her mom by wiping down the dining table, discussed tomorrow's water pipe repairs with Chuck in the language of men who understood exactly what needed to be done, and listened to Noah's excited recap of the game's highlights with patience.

This was what she'd hoped to see tonight—glimpses of the man Cade had been before life showed him the cruel side of human beings. She'd seen cracks in the armor he wore like a shield, moments when his natural warmth and humor broke through the protective barriers.

Please, God, she prayed silently, *help him find his way back to the man he used to be. Help him remember that he's worthy of love and belonging, that his heart is safe with people who truly care about him. Help him see that life is worth living to the fullest.*

Chapter 14

"Hand me that smaller wrench, partner," Chuck's voice carried from the kitchen into the dining room, followed by the metallic clink of tools and Noah's eager response of "This one, Grandpa?"

Eva paused in her wallpaper scraping to listen as her father's patient instruction mixed with Cade's quieter explanations about pipe threading and water pressure. From her position on the stepladder, she could see through the doorway to where three pairs of legs—one small, two longer—protruded from beneath the kitchen sink cabinet.

"Perfect," Cade's voice was muffled but warm. "Now hold that steady while your grandpa tightens the connection. That's it—you're getting good at this."

Ruby smiled up at Eva from where she knelt on the drop cloth, working on the lower portion of the dining room wall. "Those three make quite the team," she said, attacking a stubborn strip of adhesive with renewed vigor. "I haven't heard your dad enjoy a project this much in quite some time."

Eva returned to her scraping, though her attention remained divided between the floral wallpaper and the sound of Noah's excited chatter drifting from the kitchen. Her son was asking a million questions about pipe sizes and fitting types, his enthusiasm infectious enough to draw actual chuckles from Cade.

"Mom," she said quietly, testing the wallpaper scraper against a particularly stubborn section, "how would you help someone who's been hurt so badly they've forgotten who they used to be?"

Ruby's hands stilled on her scraper, and Eva felt her mother's perceptive gaze studying her profile. "Are we talking about someone in particular, or just speaking hypothetically?"

The gentle teasing in Ruby's voice made Eva smile despite the seriousness of her thoughts. "I'm talking about Cade," she admitted, abandoning any pretense of casual curiosity. "Last night at dinner, during the game—I saw glimpses of the man he used to be. I want to see more of that."

"And?" Ruby prompted gently.

Eva climbed down from the ladder and sank onto one of the plastic-covered chairs, suddenly needing to have this conversation face-to-face rather than calling down from her perch. Through the kitchen doorway, she could see Noah's sneakers wiggling with excitement.

"It breaks my heart to see him like this," Eva said quietly, her voice thick with emotion.

Ruby set down her scraper and reached for Eva's hand, her touch warm and steady.

"I've been thinking," Eva said, glancing toward the kitchen. "He deserves to know that he's still worthy of happiness and belonging. I still have feelings for him, Mom..."

From the kitchen came the sound of metal on metal, followed by Chuck's satisfied grunt. "That should do it. Noah, want to be the one to turn the water back on?"

"Can I really?" Noah's voice practically vibrated with excitement.

"Absolutely," Cade said. "Just remember what we talked about—turn it slowly until you hear the water running smooth."

Ruby squeezed Eva's hand gently. "I know you do. Now, what's going on in that pretty head of yours?"

Eva glanced toward the kitchen again, lowering her voice even further. "I was wondering if you might be willing to help me with a little plan I'm putting together. It's nothing pushy or crazy. Just daily things that might bring him back around... might help him come back to God."

"It worked!" Noah's triumphant shout from the kitchen interrupted their conversation, followed by the sound of running water and Chuck's approving laughter.

"Look at that—steady pressure, no leaks, and the shutoff valve works like a charm," Chuck announced. "We make a good team, gentlemen."

"The best team!" Noah agreed enthusiastically. "Cade, you're like the best fixer person ever!"

Ruby's eyes sparkled with maternal understanding as she looked at her daughter. "Okay, you know I'll help you in any way I can; tell me more."

The sound of footsteps announced the approach of their successful repair crew. Cade appeared in the dining room doorway first, wiping his hands on a work rag, his hair slightly mussed from his time spent crawling around under the sink. There was satisfaction in his posture that spoke of a job well done and time well spent.

"Kitchen sink is back in business," he announced. "New supply lines, updated shutoff valves in the kitchen and basement, and a faucet that should give you years of good service."

"Thank you," Eva said, standing up from her chair and trying not to notice how his work shirt clung to his shoulders. "I appreciate all the work you've done."

Chuck and Noah appeared behind Cade, both wearing matching grins of masculine accomplishment. Noah's shirt bore evidence of his hands-on participation in the form of pipe joint compound smudges, while Chuck carried the satisfaction of a grandfather who'd just passed along important life skills to an eager student.

"What else could we help you with while we're here?" Chuck asked, surveying the dining room's wallpaper removal progress with an approving nod. "Got our tools out and our work clothes on—might as well make the most of it."

Before Eva could suggest that they'd already done more than enough, Noah piped up with the enthusiasm that had characterized his entire morning. "Could you help me fix my bedroom?" he asked, turning to look directly at Cade with hopeful blue eyes.

Noah grabbed Cade's hand with the natural trust of childhood, his small fingers wrapping around the older man's calloused ones with complete confidence. "Please? You know all about cowboy stuff. I need a rancher room."

Eva watched Cade's face as he processed Noah's request. Surprise flickered across his features.

"Well now," Chuck said with a grin as he observed the interaction between his grandson and Cade. "Sounds like my grandson needs a proper cowboy bedroom. What do you think, Eva?"

"I say go for it," she said warmly. "Why don't you three go upstairs and figure out what needs to be done?"

Noah's whoop of excitement could probably be heard in the next county, and he immediately began tugging Cade toward the staircase with the determination of a boy who'd just been granted his dearest wish. "Come on! I want horse pictures and maybe a rope and cattle and cowboy hats!"

Cade allowed himself to be pulled along, though Eva caught the quick glance he sent in her direction—a look that seemed to ask if she was certain about this arrangement.

Eva smiled, hoping her expression conveyed the confidence she felt in him.

As the three males disappeared up the staircase amid Noah's excited planning chatter and Chuck's amused observations about eight-year-old decorating priorities, Eva turned to face her mother with anticipation sparkling in her eyes.

"Well," she said, settling back into her chair, "I'd say this is the perfect time to work on my plan while the boys can't overhear anything."

Ruby's smile was full of maternal conspiracy. "I'm all ears, sweetheart. Tell me everything you have in mind."

Chapter 15

*S*unday, *June 14th...*

The steady rhythm of sandpaper against wood provided a meditation that Cade had come to depend on during his Sunday afternoons. With the garage door rolled open to let in the fresh Montana air and a classic country station playing softly from his old radio, he worked on the piece that had been occupying his spare time for the past month—a hope chest.

Cade paused to examine his progress, running his fingers along the smooth grain where he'd been working out an imperfection in the wood. The craftsmanship wasn't perfect, but there was something satisfying about creating something beautiful from raw materials, something that would last long after the maker was forgotten.

The distant sound of an engine approaching made him look up from his work. Visitors were rare, especially on Sunday afternoons when most folks were either resting after church or spending time with their families. He assumed it was Chuck, probably wanting to discuss the week's schedule or some issue with the cattle that couldn't wait until Monday morning.

Cade set down his sandpaper and stepped out of the garage, wiping his hands on the work rag tucked into his back pocket. But instead of Chuck's blue pickup, he watched Eva's SUV navigate the gravel drive toward his cabin. She parked and climbed out of the vehicle. The sight of her nearly knocked the breath from his lungs.

She was dressed for church. A pink flowered dress that somehow managed to be both modest and utterly feminine, paired with a matching hat that cast delicate shadows across her face and heels that made her legs look impossibly long. She moved with the grace of a woman who knew who she was and was comfortable in her own skin.

Noah bounced out of the passenger side. He, too, was dressed in his Sunday best—khaki pants, a button-down shirt, and a tie that was slightly askew despite what had clearly been his mother's best efforts.

"Cade!" Noah called out as he skipped toward the garage. "Pastor Sam told us about David and Goliath and how David wasn't afraid!"

"Sounds interesting," Cade managed, though his attention kept drifting to Eva, who was walking toward him with something in her hands and an expression that seemed almost nervous.

"Pastor Sam said faith is like a muscle—the more you use it, the stronger it gets. And he said... he said... I'm having a hard time rememberin'."

"Noah," Eva said, "take a breath, son. And then apologize for us intruding on Mr. Mayer today."

"Cade," he corrected automatically. "And you're not bothering me. I was just working on a project."

Eva's gaze shifted toward the open garage door, curiosity flickering across her features. "A project? What kind of project?"

"Just some woodworking," he said. "Nothing fancy."

Eva walked inside, her heels clicking softly on the concrete floor as she took in the organized chaos of his hobby. Tools hung neatly on pegboard walls, lumber was stacked according to type and size, and his current project sat on the workbench under the focused beam of an adjustable lamp.

"Oh my," she breathed, moving toward the partially completed chest. "Cade, this is beautiful."

"Still working on it," he said, following her into the garage and trying not to notice how the soft lighting made her skin glow or how her perfume mixed with the scent of wood shavings to create something that made his head spin. "It's just a hobby. Keeps my hands busy."

Eva ran her fingers along the smooth wood, tracing the grain. "The detail is incredible. What's it going to be when it's finished?"

"A hope chest."

"It's going to be gorgeous. Someone's going to treasure this forever."

Noah had wandered over to examine Cade's tool collection. "Could you teach me to make stuff?" he asked, his eyes bright with possibility.

"If your mom thinks it's a good idea."

"We'll see," Eva said. "Let's do what we came to and let Cade enjoy his afternoon."

"This is for you," Eva continued, extending a gift bag to him. "Just a little something we picked up in town after church."

Cade accepted the bag with confusion, looking from Eva to Noah and back again. "You didn't need to—"

"It's nothing... really," Eva interrupted, her cheeks flushing pink in a way that made her even more beautiful. "Just enjoy it when you have time."

Cade looked inside the bag and withdrew a loaf of banana bread wrapped in clear cellophane. A folded piece of paper was attached to the wrapping with a small ribbon, and he looked up at Eva with questions in his eyes.

"Read the note later," she said quickly, taking Noah's hand with obvious intention to leave.

But Noah had other plans. As Eva began to guide him toward their vehicle, he dug in his heels and turned back to face Cade with the determination of a boy who'd just remembered something important.

"Will you take me horseback riding?" Noah asked. "You said maybe before...."

"Noah," Eva said quickly, her face flushing with embarrassment, "we can't just show up and expect—"

"Horseback riding," Cade interrupted, considering the request. The afternoon was beautiful, and he'd been planning to check on the horses, anyway. "Today... well, I suppose I have time if your mom's okay with it."

Noah turned to look at his mother with hopeful blue eyes that would have melted stone. "Mom, you come too. Please?"

Eva glanced back and forth between her son and Cade.

"Come on, Eva," Cade said. "When's the last time you went riding?"

Eva hesitated for a moment longer, then smiled with the kind of genuine happiness that transformed her entire face. "We'd need to change out of our church clothes first."

"Take your time. I'll head down to the barn and get a couple of horses saddled. Meet me there when you're ready."

As Eva and Noah climbed back into their SUV, Cade caught Noah's excited chatter about which horse he hoped to ride and Eva's gentle reminders about safety and following instructions. He watched them drive away.

Standing alone in his driveway, Cade looked down at the gift bag in his hands and carefully unfolded the note attached to the banana bread. Eva's handwriting was neat and feminine, and the words she'd chosen made his breath catch in his throat:

"Trust in the Lord with all your heart and lean not on your own understanding; in all your ways submit to him, and he will make your paths straight." - Proverbs 3:5-6

For a long moment, Cade stared at the verse. He'd read those words countless times and had even believed them once upon a time when faith had seemed as natural as breathing.

Cade folded the note carefully and slipped it into his shirt pocket.

Chapter 16

"I hope you haven't eaten lunch yet," Eva called out as she and Noah entered the barn. She held up a small insulated bag with a grin. "We haven't, and we thought maybe we could take a break somewhere along our ride and eat together."

Cade looked up from adjusting the stirrups on a gentle bay mare, taking in Eva's transformed appearance with an expression she couldn't quite read. She'd changed from her church dress into comfortable jeans, paired with a soft lavender blouse and riding boots. Her hair was pulled back in a ponytail, and she'd traded her Sunday hat for a well-worn baseball cap.

"Sounds good."

Noah bounced on his toes beside Eva, wearing jeans, a Western shirt, and the small pair of boots Chuck had bought him for Christmas. "Is that Buttercup?"

"It is. She's one of the most gentle horses on the ranch," Cade confirmed, giving the mare's neck an affectionate pat. "I figured you and your mom would enjoy riding on her."

"Can I ride with you on Storm instead?" Noah asked.

"If your mom's okay with it," Cade said, glancing toward Eva.

"Sounds good to me."

Cade moved to help Eva mount Buttercup first, his hands steady and sure as he held the stirrup and offered his shoulder for balance. The brief contact when his fingers brushed hers made electricity shoot up her arm, and Eva had to concentrate harder than necessary to settle gracefully into the saddle.

"Thank you," she managed, trying to ignore the way Cade's closeness made her pulse quicken.

"Anytime."

Eva watched with a mixture of pride and tenderness as Cade lifted her son, settling him in front of the saddle horn on Storm's back. The big bay gelding stood perfectly still during the process.

"You can help me, Noah. Hold the reins lightly, keep your heels down, and trust Storm to do most of the work." Cade said as he swung up behind Noah with fluid grace.

"I remember," Noah said solemnly, though his excitement was barely contained.

As they rode out of the barn into the brilliant afternoon sunshine, Eva felt a sense of rightness settle over her like a warm blanket. The Montana landscape stretched endlessly before them—rolling pastures dotted with wildflowers, the distant peaks of the Sapphire Mountains creating a dramatic backdrop, and the vast blue sky that seemed to go on forever.

"Where would you like to go?" Cade asked, guiding Storm alongside Buttercup as they followed the well-worn trail that led away from the ranch buildings.

"Surprise me," Eva said, tilting her face toward the sun.

Cade was quiet for a moment. "How about the creek?" he suggested. "It's a good spot for lunch."

The mention of the creek sent a cascade of memories through Eva's mind—summer afternoons spent exploring its banks, teenage conversations about dreams and the future, and stolen kisses under the cottonwood trees that lined its shores. It had been one of their favorite places, a peaceful sanctuary where they could escape the expectations of parents and teachers and just be themselves.

"The creek sounds perfect."

They rode for a while, with only the sounds of hoofbeats and Noah's occasional excited observations about the wildlife they spotted along the way. Eva stole glances at Cade, noting the patient manner in which he answered Noah's endless questions and the gradual relaxation in his posture as they moved farther from the ranch buildings.

This was the Cade she remembered, the man who came alive outdoors, who found peace in the rhythm of riding and the vastness of the Montana sky.

When they reached the creek, Eva's breath caught at the sight of the gentle water cascading over smooth stones, creating natural pools perfect for wading, and the gentle music that had been the soundtrack to so many of her happiest memories. Cottonwood trees provided shade, while wildflowers carpeted the banks in brilliant splashes of color.

They dismounted and settled on a large, smooth boulder that overlooked the water, the horses grazing contentedly nearby. Eva unpacked their simple lunch—peanut butter and jelly sandwiches, apple slices, and homemade cookies that Noah immediately declared the best part of the meal.

"Can I wade in the creek?" Noah asked around a mouthful of sandwich, his eyes bright with anticipation as he watched the water sparkle in the afternoon sunlight.

"If you're careful and stay in the shallow parts... finish your sandwich," Eva said.

Noah wolfed down his sandwich with impressive speed, then kicked off his boots and socks with the enthusiasm of a boy who'd just been granted access to paradise. But as he started toward the water's edge, Eva called him back.

"Hold on there, cowboy," she said with a laugh. "Let me roll up those pants legs, or you'll have wet jeans for the rest of the afternoon."

Noah submitted with barely contained patience, bouncing on his toes while Eva rolled his jeans to his knees. The moment she finished, he was off like a shot, splashing into the shallow water with whoops of delight that echoed off the surrounding hills.

Eva settled back onto the rock beside Cade, tucking her legs beneath her as she watched Noah explore the creek with the fearless curiosity of childhood. The afternoon sun was warm on her shoulders, and the peaceful sounds of the water and her son's laughter as he romped in the creek created a symphony that eased something deep in her soul.

"He's a good kid," Cade said, his attention focused on Noah as the boy crouched down to examine something fascinating in the creek bed.

"He is," Eva agreed, pride and love evident in her voice. "Sometimes I worry that I'm not enough for him, though."

Cade turned to look at her, and Eva was surprised by the intensity in his eyes. "It seems you've done a great job with him, Eva. Noah's confident, curious and kind—that doesn't happen accidentally."

"That means a lot, especially coming from you."

"Tell me about Bozeman. What made you decide to come back home?"

Eva considered how much to share and how honest to be about the loneliness and dissatisfaction that had driven her back to Riverbend Valley. "I wasn't happy anymore. Teaching wasn't what I thought it would be," she said finally. "Too much politics, too little time actually working with kids. I felt like I was drowning in paperwork and standardized tests instead of nurturing young minds."

"That must have been frustrating."

"It was. And Noah was starting to ask questions about why we couldn't visit my mom and dad more often, why we couldn't have a dog, why our apartment was so small..." Eva's voice trailed off as she remembered her son's wistful remarks about the differences between city life and the ranch. "I realized I was holding onto a life that wasn't really working for either of us."

"So you came home."

"So I came home," Eva confirmed, glancing around at the peaceful beauty that surrounded them.

Noah's voice called out from the creek, interrupting their conversation.

"Cade! Come look!" Noah shouted excitedly, holding up something that glittered in the afternoon sunlight. "I found gold!"

Cade stood up, kicking off his boots and pulling off his socks with the easy movements of someone who'd never quite outgrown the appeal of creek exploration. Eva watched as he rolled up his jeans and waded into the shallow water to join Noah, his attention focused entirely on the treasure he'd discovered.

"Now this is special," she heard Cade say as he crouched down beside Noah. "See how it catches the light? It's probably mica—it's what makes some rocks sparkle like that."

Noah's delighted laughter drifted across the water as he and Cade continued their exploration.

"Mom!" Noah called out after a few minutes. "Come join us!"

Eva hesitated for a moment, aware that joining them would complete some kind of picture she wasn't sure she was ready to embrace. But the afternoon was beautiful, Noah's happiness was infectious, and something about the way Cade looked at her—patient and hopeful and entirely without pressure—made the decision for her.

She slipped off her boots and socks, rolled up her jeans, and waded into the creek with a grin. The water was perfect—cool enough to be refreshing but warmed by the afternoon sun, with a sandy bottom that felt wonderful beneath her bare feet.

"This creek brings back good memories," she said to Cade as she watched Noah continue his enthusiastic exploration a few feet away.

"That it does," he said quietly.

Chapter 17

Cade parked his truck beside the foreman's cabin, the engine ticking softly as it cooled in the evening air. He sat for a moment, letting the quiet settle around him after a long day of moving cattle to fresh pasture. His shoulders ached from hours in the saddle, and dust from the range had worked its way into every crease of his clothing, but there was satisfaction in the exhaustion that came from honest work.

The ranch hands had been in good spirits today, joking and telling stories as they worked, and Chuck had complimented him on the efficiency of the cattle rotation system he'd implemented. It should have been enough—the steady paycheck, the respect of his employer, and the knowledge that he was good at what he did. For months, it had been enough, providing the structure and purpose that kept him moving forward one day at a time.

But something had shifted since yesterday afternoon at the creek, and Cade found himself thinking about Eva's laughter as she waded into the shallow water, the way Noah had looked at him with such obvious trust and affection, and the comfortable ease of sharing a simple meal while watching the boy explore with boundless curiosity.

Cade climbed out of the truck and headed toward his front porch, already planning the evening's routine—shower, dinner, and maybe some work on the hope chest if his hands weren't too tired.

As he climbed the wooden steps of his porch, something white caught his eye, tucked between the screen door and the door frame like a small flag of surrender.

He pulled the paper free and unfolded it, recognizing Eva's neat handwriting:

"Forget the former things; do not dwell on the past. See, I am doing a new thing..."- Isaiah 43:18-19

You might not see it yet, but I believe something good is still ahead for you. - Me

Cade stared at the verse until the words blurred slightly, his throat tightening with an emotion he couldn't name. The biblical passage hit him with the force of a physical blow, addressing directly the thing he'd been struggling with for months—the inability to move beyond the devastation Rachel had left in her wake, the constant replay of failures and betrayals that kept him trapped in a past that offered nothing but pain.

Forget the former things; do not dwell on the past.

It sounded so simple when reduced to black ink on white paper, but Cade knew the reality was infinitely more complex. How did a man forget the destruction of everything he'd had? How could a man stop dwelling on a marriage that had cost him his ranch?

See, I am doing a new thing.

The promise felt both impossible and desperately needed, like water offered to a man dying of thirst in the desert.

I believe something good is still ahead for you.

Not might be, not could be, but a statement of faith in possibilities he'd stopped allowing himself to consider.

Eva saw something in him that he'd forgotten existed and believed in a future he'd convinced himself was beyond reach.

Cade folded the note and slipped it into his shirt pocket. He turned and looked toward the bed and breakfast, where warm light glowed in the windows like a beacon of welcome. Eva was probably preparing dinner for herself and Noah or maybe reviewing plans for the B&B's restoration.

You might not see it yet, but I believe something good is still ahead for you.

Cade turned away from the view of the bed and breakfast and headed inside his cabin.

Chapter 18

Tuesday, June 16th...

As Cade climbed the porch steps, he noticed a small brown bag sitting on one of his wooden rocking chairs. He scanned the area as if Eva might materialize from behind a tree with that gentle smile that had been haunting his thoughts for days.

Three days.

Three unexpected gestures.

He picked it up and looked inside.

A small plastic container held homemade chocolate chip cookies. Taped to the lid was another folded piece of paper. He peeled it away and opened it.

"The Lord is close to the brokenhearted and saves those who are crushed in spirit." – Psalm 34:18

I came across this and smiled. He hasn't left you—not once. – Just thought you should know

Cade sank into the rocking chair and balanced the container of cookies on his knees as he read the verse again.

The Lord is close to the brokenhearted.

Saves those who are crushed in spirit.

Cade opened the container and took out one of the cookies. The cookie was perfect—crispy edges, soft center, and just the right balance of sweetness.

As he sat rocking slowly on his porch, the evening air soft around him and Eva's words of hope pressed close to his heart, Cade looked toward the bed and breakfast. He could see Eva's silhouette moving around inside.

The urge to walk over and thank her for the cookies and ask her out to dinner was almost overwhelming.

What if he was misreading her intentions? What if the cookies and Bible verses were simple Christian charity rather than personal interest? What if he knocked on her door and found that the ease they'd shared during their horseback ride was harder to recapture when it wasn't buffered by Noah's innocent enthusiasm?

Caring for Eva meant risking the kind of devastation he'd barely survived once before and meant believing that love could be something other than a weapon used to destroy the very foundations of a man's life.

He folded Eva's note and slipped it into his shirt pocket.

He stood up from the rocking chair, taking the container of cookies with him as he headed toward his front door. But before he went inside, he allowed himself one more long look toward the bed and breakfast.

Chapter 19

Wednesday, June 17th…

Cade pulled his pickup into its usual spot beside the foreman's cabin. Storm clouds had been building over the Sapphire Mountains all afternoon, promising the kind of summer thunderstorm that would either bring blessed relief from the heat or create muddy complications for tomorrow's work, depending on how hard the rain decided to fall.

He'd spent the day helping Chuck move cattle to higher pasture, work that required careful attention to both terrain and temperament as they guided the cattle through gates and along fence lines toward better grazing. The physical demands of the job had kept his mind occupied for most of the day, but during the quiet moments his thoughts had wandered inevitably to Eva.

Cade climbed out of his truck and headed toward the porch. He looked around for whatever token Eva had left today with the expectation of someone who'd learned to anticipate good things. He spotted a white envelope lying on the porch directly in front of his screen door.

He bent to pick up the envelope. The weight of the envelope suggested it contained more than just another folded verse, and Cade's pulse quickened as he carefully tore open the sealed flap.

Inside was indeed a folded piece of paper, but also something that made him pause—a photograph. The image showed him and Eva on their graduation day, both wearing the blue caps and gowns that had marked their passage from high school to the uncertain territory of adulthood. But it wasn't the formal ceremony that the photographer had captured—it was a spontaneous moment, both of them caught mid-laugh as they faced each other with expressions of pure joy.

Cade stared at the photograph, remembering with startling clarity the moment it had been taken. Eva had just whispered something about Principal Morrison's toupee moving independently during his commencement speech, and Cade had responded with an equally irreverent observation about the superintendent's unfortunate choice of tie. The shared laughter had bubbled up between them with the easy intimacy of two people who'd learned each other's sense of humor, who could find comedy in situations that others took entirely seriously.

They looked so young in the picture, so confident that the future spread out before them like an uncharted territory full of adventure and possibility. Eva's smile was radiant beneath her graduation cap, and Cade could see in his expression was the kind of unguarded happiness that he'd forgotten he was capable of feeling.

With hands that weren't quite steady, he unfolded Eva's note and read the message:

"A cheerful heart is good medicine, but a crushed spirit dries up the bones." – Proverbs 17:22

Laughter looked good on you then, and I know it still will now.

The crushed spirit the proverb described was an accurate diagnosis of his condition.

But Eva's personal message suggested she saw past his current darkness to the man he'd been before life taught him that happiness was a luxury he couldn't afford.

Laughter looked good on you then, and I know it still will now.

The confidence in those words was both a gift and a challenge, an expression of faith in his capacity for healing that he didn't share but desperately wanted to believe. Eva wasn't just offering sympathy for his wounds—she was insisting that those wounds didn't define him, that the man in the graduation photograph was still there beneath all the layers of protective numbness he'd accumulated.

Cade sank onto his porch steps, the photograph in one hand while he read the verse again. The approaching storm had brought an early twilight, and the first rumbles of thunder rolled across the valley like a distant conversation between the mountains and sky. He should go inside, eat dinner, and call it a day.

Instead, he studied the graduation photograph and remembered not just that moment of shared laughter but the entire day that had marked both an ending and a beginning in ways they hadn't fully understood at the time. They'd been so certain that their love could survive anything, so confident that the connection between them was strong enough to bridge whatever distance college might create.

In some ways, they'd been naive about the challenges that lay ahead, about how easily even the strongest bonds could be strained by time and circumstance and the gradual accumulation of experiences that pulled people in different directions. But in other ways, maybe they'd been wiser than their older selves gave them credit for—maybe the laughter captured in that photograph was worth preserving, worth fighting for, worth believing in even when life provided countless reasons for cynicism.

The first fat raindrops began to fall as Cade sat on his porch steps, creating dark spots on the wooden steps and filling the air with the rich scent of an approaching storm. He tucked the photo in the envelope and set it behind him on the porch to protect it from the rain. He folded the note and tucked it in his pocket.

The urge to walk across the distance between his cabin and the bed and breakfast was stronger tonight. The photograph had awakened memories of who he'd been when he believed in possibilities, when laughter came easily, and when love felt like an adventure rather than a risk.

Eva's lights were on, warm, and welcoming against the gathering darkness. She was so close, just a few minutes' walk across familiar ground, close enough that he could knock on her door and thank her for the photograph and could tell her that her daily messages were reaching him in ways she might not realize.

The rain began to fall in earnest, creating a gentle drumbeat on the cabin's metal roof and washing the air clean with the kind of summer storm that promised new growth and fresh beginnings.

He stood up from the porch steps and took one long look toward the bed and breakfast. Tomorrow, he told himself. Tomorrow he might find the courage to do more than just accept her gifts with grateful silence.

Shaking his head, Cade headed inside his cabin as the storm settled over the valley with the kind of cleansing power that sometimes made all things new.

Chapter 20

Thursday, June 18th...

Cade put his truck in park and scanned his front porch.

Sure enough, there was a white piece of paper tucked between his screen door and the door frame.

He grinned.

Five days.

Five consecutive gestures. The sheer determination required to maintain such consistent kindness with no word or acknowledgement from him was both humbling and slightly overwhelming.

Cade climbed out of his truck and climbed the porch steps. He reached for the note, unfolded it and read:

"Do not fear, for I am with you... I will strengthen you and help you."
– Isaiah 41:10

Life doesn't always make sense. But sometimes, the best things rise in the dark. You don't have to see the whole road—just take the next step. – With faith enough for both of us

Cade placed his hand against the cabin wall, bracing himself as the full impact of five days of accumulated kindness settled over him like a weight he wasn't sure he was strong enough to carry. Each message had been carefully chosen to address a specific aspect of his wounds—his lost faith, his sense of abandonment, his inability to imagine joy, his crushing shame about the past. Eva had been systematically dismantling his reasons for despair with the precision of someone who understood exactly what needed healing.

He read the note again, letting the words sink deeper into his consciousness. The woman who'd written these words wasn't offering casual comfort or obligatory Christian charity—she was making a deliberate investment in his restoration, betting her own emotional energy on the possibility that love could indeed triumph over betrayal.

Do not fear, for I am with you.

Cade folded the note and slipped it into his shirt pocket.

As Cade stood there wrestling with hope and fear in equal measure, one thought rose above all the others with startling clarity: *She's not giving up on me.*

Chapter 21

Friday, June 19th...

Cade's truck coughed to a stop in front of his cabin, the engine's complaint echoing his frustration with a day that had tested every ounce of his patience. Nine-fifteen. The dashboard clock glowed accusingly in the darkness, confirming what his aching shoulders and empty stomach already knew—this had been one of those days when Murphy's Law reigned supreme and everything that could go wrong had taken turns making his life miserable.

The heat had been oppressive from dawn to dusk, the kind of muggy Montana weather that made both man and beast irritable. The morning had started with a broken water pump in the south pasture, which led to an emergency run to town for parts, which led to discovering that the part they needed was on back order, which led to rigging a temporary solution that held just long enough for the afternoon thunderstorm to knock out power to the main barn.

By the time they'd gotten the generator running and checked every head of cattle twice, the sun was setting and Cade's patience was worn thinner than old denim. Chuck had finally sent him home with strict orders to get some rest.

The porch was dark, and Cade had to use his phone's flashlight to navigate the steps. The white paper tucked between his screen door and the frame should have brought comfort, but tonight he was almost too tired to care about scripture verses and encouraging words.

Almost.

He pulled the note free and unlocked his door. Inside, he dropped heavily into his recliner and rubbed his eyes with the heels of his hands before unfolding Eva's message.

"For I know the plans I have for you... plans to give you hope and a future." – Jeremiah 29:11

Come down to Mom and Dad's house tomorrow around 5 for a cookout. Just bring yourself; Mom and I are going shopping tomorrow for food. Noah hopes you'll come... fair warning... he wants you to teach him how to play horseshoes.

Cade stared at the note, reading it twice to make sure his tired mind hadn't misunderstood the words. For six days, Eva had been sending him scripture and encouragement. But today's message was different.

This was an invitation.

The verse itself was familiar—he'd heard it countless times in Sunday school and church services. But tonight, after a day when every plan had gone sideways and every solution had created new problems, the promise felt both foreign and desperately needed.

Plans to give you hope and a future.

Hope. The word that had been absent from his vocabulary for so long that seeing it in print felt like encountering a foreign language.

Eva's personal message suggested she believed in those plans and was actively working to help them unfold.

Come down to Mom and Dad's house tomorrow around 5 for a cookout.

Simple words that carried enormous weight.

Just bring yourself.

Those three words hit him harder than the scripture verse. In a world where his value seemed tied to what he could provide—his skills, his labor, his usefulness—Eva was asking for nothing more than his presence. She didn't need him to fix anything or solve any problems or prove his worth through competence. She just wanted him there.

Noah hopes you'll come... fair warning... he wants you to teach him how to play horseshoes.

Despite his exhaustion, Cade felt his mouth quirk upward at the image of Noah's eager face. The warning was unnecessary—spending time with Noah had become one of the unexpected pleasures of Eva's return, a reminder of what it felt like to be someone's hero for purely innocent reasons.

Cade folded the note, got up, and walked to his dining table, where a wooden box sat. He'd made the box himself during the long winter months before Eva's return, back when his evenings stretched endlessly, and working with his hands was the only thing that kept despair at bay.

Opening the hinged lid, he placed tonight's message inside with the other five notes Eva had left for him, creating a small collection of promises and encouragement that had become more valuable to him than any treasure he could imagine. The graduation photograph lay on the table beside the box, and Cade picked it up.

Eva was systematically dismantling his reasons for avoiding her.

"Cookout," he said aloud to the empty cabin, the word feeling strange and wonderful on his tongue. "Tomorrow evening." He set the photograph down beside the wooden box and shook his head in amazement at the woman who refused to leave him alone.

"What are you doing to me, Eva?"

Chapter 22

*S*aturday, June 20th...

The morning air was crisp and clean as Cade guided Storm along the trails that crisscrossed Lost Creek Ranch, the kind of perfect Montana morning that reminded him why he'd never seriously considered leaving this valley despite all the heartbreak it had witnessed. The early sun painted the rolling pastures in shades of gold and green, while the distant peaks of the Sapphire Mountains stood sharp against a sky so blue it almost hurt to look at directly.

Storm moved beneath him with the easy rhythm of a horse who knew these trails as well as his rider did, requiring minimal guidance as they followed the fence line toward the section of grazing land where the breeding stock had been moved earlier in the week. Cade had needed this morning ride more than he'd initially realized—the peaceful solitude helping to quiet the restless energy that had kept him awake most of the night, wrestling with thoughts of Eva's invitation.

Yesterday's frustrations seemed smaller in the vastness of open country. As they completed their circuit and headed back towards home, Cade allowed Storm to set the pace. As they approached his cabin, a brown bag sitting on one of his rocking chairs caught his attention.

Seven days.

Seven consecutive days.

Cade dismounted and led Storm toward the porch, the horse following willingly as they approached the steps. Inside the bag was a plastic container still warm to the touch, and when Cade lifted the lid, the rich scent of fresh-baked blueberry muffins made his stomach growl with appreciation. He'd skipped breakfast in his eagerness to get out on the trail, and the prospect of Eva's baking was more appealing than anything he could have prepared for himself.

A folded note was taped to the container's lid, and Cade peeled it away.

"Be strong and courageous... for the Lord your God is with you wherever you go." – Joshua 1:9

Even if you don't feel him yet—God hasn't gone anywhere. See you at the cookout this evening. Don't make me come up here after you. – Still believing in you

Cade chuckled.

Don't make me come up here after you.

He folded the note and slipped it into his shirt pocket, then settled on his porch step with the container of muffins. The first bite was perfect—sweet and tender with bursts of blueberry.

As he ate, his gaze drifted toward the bed and breakfast, where movement in the backyard caught his attention. Eva and Noah had emerged from the house, both dressed casually in jeans and t-shirts. Noah began chasing his mother around the large oak tree, his laughter carrying faintly across the distance like music.

Eva was running with the exaggerated stumbling steps that adults used when playing with children, staying just ahead of Noah's reaching hands while clearly letting him think he might actually catch her. Her hair flew behind her in the morning sunlight, and her laughter mixed with her son's to create a symphony of joy.

Suddenly, Noah made a diving tackle that brought them both tumbling to the ground in a tangle of arms and legs.

The scene was so perfectly domestic, so filled with the kind of easy affection that made a house into a home, that Cade felt his throat tighten with longing. This was what he'd once dreamed of—mornings filled with laughter and play, children who looked at him with unconditional love, and a wife who found joy in simple moments rather than constantly measuring their life against some impossible standard of success.

Storm's soft whinny drew his attention away from the touching family scene, and Cade looked over to find the horse watching him.

"What?" Cade asked, genuinely curious about the expression in his horse's dark eyes.

Storm nodded his head up and down with deliberate emphasis, as if offering commentary on the situation that any fool should be able to understand.

"You think I should go to that cookout tonight, don't you?" he asked Storm, who responded by staring at him while he munched on a mouthful of grass.

Chapter 23

The sizzle of hamburger patties on the grill provided a satisfying soundtrack to what Eva hoped would be a perfect evening. She stood on the concrete patio below the back porch, spatula in hand, watching the meat brown while the aroma of charcoal and seasoning drifted up to mix with the sweet scent of honeysuckle that climbed the porch railings. Above her, Chuck, Ruby, and Noah sat in comfortable porch chairs, glasses of sweet tea sweating as they enjoyed the kind of lazy Saturday evening that made summer in Montana feel like a gift.

"Mom, I'm starving," Noah called down from his perch

"Just a few more minutes, sweetheart," Eva replied, flipping the patties.

"Cade!" Noah shouted suddenly.

Eva turned and watched Cade walk around the side of the house, looking hesitant. He wore dark Wranglers and a black polo shirt that fit perfectly. He'd clearly made an effort for the occasion, and the sight of him actually showing up put a smile on her face.

Noah launched down the porch steps. He hit Cade at full speed, wrapping his arms around the man's legs in a hug so fierce and unexpected that Cade actually staggered backward a step.

"You came! You really came!" Noah exclaimed, his words tumbling over each other in excitement. "Wait till you see my room! Mom and I painted. It looks so cool... Grandma and Grandpa brought over all kinds of cowboy stuff—a rope... pictures of horses... a cool lamp that looks like a boot, and—"

"Noah," Eva called out with a laugh, watching Cade's stunned expression as he processed the enthusiastic greeting. "Breathe, honey."

Cade's hands had settled gently on Noah's shoulders, and Eva caught the way his expression softened as he looked down at her son. "Sounds like you've been busy this week," he said, his voice making Eva's heart skip.

"I helped with everything—painting and moving furniture. Mom said I was a really good helper, didn't you, Mom?"

"The best helper I've ever had," Eva confirmed, watching as Cade lifted his gaze to meet hers.

"Evening, Chuck. Ruby," Cade said, nodding to her parents.

"Good to see you, son," Chuck replied with genuine pleasure. "Been looking forward to this all week."

"Dinner's almost ready," Ruby added with a welcoming smile. "Eva's been fussing over those hamburgers like they're made of gold."

Cade walked over to the patio where Eva stood, Noah still chattering beside him about the various improvements to his room. "Need any help?"

Eva felt a flutter of awareness at his proximity, the scent of his cologne had her pulse quicken. "Sure," she said, handing him the spatula. "Could you watch these for a minute? They're almost done, and I'll help Mom bring out the rest of the food."

Cade accepted the spatula, and Eva lingered for a moment.

"Still like yours, well done?" he asked, glancing at her.

"You better believe it," Eva replied with a grin. As she started to turn toward the porch steps, his voice stopped her.

"The blueberry muffins were good."

Eva felt her smile widen at the simple acknowledgment. "I'm glad you enjoyed them," she said, then headed up the steps to help her mom.

In the kitchen, Ruby was loading a tray with all the accompaniments that made a proper cookout—sliced tomatoes and onions, pickles, three different kinds of cheese, and a basket of fresh hamburger buns from the bakery in town.

"He came," Ruby said with satisfaction, glancing out the window toward where Cade stood tending the grill with Noah as his enthusiastic assistant.

"He sure did."

"He's a good man. Always has been."

Eva nodded, watching through the window as Cade listened patiently to Noah's running commentary. There was something about the way he interacted with her son that made her throat tighten with emotion.

"What are you thinking about?"

Eva looked at her mom and smiled. "I'm thinking I'm right where I need to be. And... I believe God brought me home for more than I originally thought."

Ruby smiled and looked outside at her grandson smiling up at Cade. "Does it bother you how attached Noah's getting?"

"Not in the least."

Ruby turned to her daughter and said, "Eva, I hope you know your daddy and I are always happy to watch Noah… you know… if you ever want to go out on a proper date."

"I may just take you up on that, but not just yet."

They carried the food out to the porch table just as Cade was bringing up the tray of cooked hamburgers, Noah trailing behind him like an eager apprentice.

"Smells wonderful," Ruby declared as they arranged everything on the table.

When they were all seated around the table, Chuck offered a simple blessing that encompassed the food, the fellowship, and the gratitude for being together.

The conversation that followed was the kind that Eva had been hoping for—easy and inclusive, with Cade relaxing and enjoying himself. He asked Chuck about the ranch's plans for the summer cattle rotation, complimented Ruby on the potato salad that had always been his favorite, and listened with genuine interest as Noah continued his detailed description of his new bedroom.

"And the best part," Noah said around a bite of hamburger, "Grandpa gave me this really cool hat rack that looks like a horse. I can hang my cowboy hat on it just like a real rancher."

"Sounds like you're all set," Cade said with a smile, tugging at the corners of his mouth.

Several times during dinner she caught Cade watching her with an intensity that made her pulse quicken, and each time when their eyes met, he didn't look away.

As they finished eating and settled into the comfortable lethargy that followed a good meal, Noah suddenly straightened with renewed energy.

"Cade, will you teach me to play horseshoes now?" he asked.

"Only if your mom plays," he said with a grin that transformed his entire face.

"Please, Mom?" Noah added, bouncing slightly in his chair.

"Of course, honey," she said as she stood. "I wouldn't miss this for anything."

Chapter 24

"**A**nd that's how you throw a ringer!" Eva announced triumphantly as her horseshoe clanged around the metal stake with satisfying precision, earning her a whoop of celebration from Noah and an appreciative nod from Cade.

"Mom, you're really good," Noah said, and Eva could hear the exhaustion creeping into his voice. The evening had been perfect—two hours of horseshoes instruction that had involved far more laughter than actual skill development, with Cade patiently teaching Noah the proper stance and throwing technique while Eva provided comic relief with her wildly inconsistent aim.

"I think I had luck on my side this evening, son," Eva replied.

Cade gathered the horseshoes before they walked back toward the house.

"Look, Grandpa's starting a fire," Noah said, pointing toward where Chuck was crouched beside the stone fire pit behind the house.

"Can we make s'mores?" Noah asked, turning to Eva with hopeful eyes that still sparkled despite his obvious tiredness.

Eva glanced toward the fire pit where the first flames were beginning to catch, then up toward the porch where Ruby was emerging with a tray loaded with all the necessary s'mores supplies. Her mother's timing was impeccable, as always.

"I suppose we could," Eva said with a smile, then looked up at Cade. "Will you stay?"

For a moment, Cade's expression showed the same careful consideration that had characterized most of his interactions since her return. But then Noah slipped his small hand into Cade's larger one with the unconscious trust of childhood.

"For a little while," he said.

They settled around the fire pit as Chuck coaxed the flames higher, a circle of Adirondack chairs positioned around it. Cade chose the chair next to Eva's.

Ruby distributed roasting sticks, while Chuck helped Noah select the perfect marshmallow and demonstrated the patient rotation technique needed for even browning.

"Slow and steady," Chuck instructed as Noah held his stick over the fire with intense concentration. "The secret is not gettin' in a hurry."

Eva studied Cade's profile in the flickering firelight, noting the way the dancing flames caught the silver threads at his temples and softened the lines that spoke of too much worry and not enough laughter.

He caught her looking and asked, "How are things going with the bed and breakfast?"

"Good," Eva replied. "I finished stripping all the wallpaper in the dining room, hallway, and parlor. I was able to paint the dining room this week. I built a simple website, and it's live on the internet now. Tomorrow I'm planning to tackle painting the parlor."

"Have you started advertising yet?"

"I've got three reservations for September already, all from people who stayed with Aunt Connie before and heard through the grapevine that I was reopening. It's encouraging."

"It's going to be wonderful, honey. Just you wait, the more word spreads, the better," Ruby said from across the fire.

"I hope so. But really, I'm not all that worried about it. I'm confident that in time, I'll have steady reservations," Eva said.

Cade nodded thoughtfully, his gaze fixed on the dancing flames. "I hope you stay so busy you have to hire help."

The conversation flowed as naturally as the creek that ran behind the house, touching on everything from Noah's excitement over registering for vacation Bible School that would start in late July to Chuck's plans for expanding the cattle operation. Eva shared stories about her teaching years in Bozeman—the frustrations and joys of working with children and the gradual realization that her heart was calling her home.

"I kept telling myself I was building a career," she said, accepting a perfectly toasted marshmallow from Noah and sandwiching it between graham crackers and chocolate. "But I was really just marking time until I could figure out what I actually wanted to do with my life."

"And now you know?" Cade asked.

Eva looked around the circle—at her parents sharing quiet conversation, at Noah, whose enthusiasm for s'mores was beginning to give way to drowsiness, and at Cade, whose attention was focused entirely on her with an intensity that made her pulse quicken.

"Now I know," she confirmed.

As the fire settled into a steady burn and the evening deepened around them, Eva gathered her courage for the question she'd been wanting to ask all week.

"Would you like to come to church with us tomorrow?" she asked, trying to keep her voice casual despite the hope that made her heart race.

Cade looked down at his hands, and Eva watched his shoulders tense. "Not yet," he said, his voice rough.

The disappointment was sharp but not unexpected. "I understand," she said gently, meaning it.

Noah chose that moment to climb into Eva's lap, his head settling against her chest with the boneless exhaustion of a child who'd packed too much excitement into one day. Eva wrapped her arms around him automatically, pressing a kiss to his sandy hair.

"Someone's getting tired," she said with a soft laugh, feeling Noah's weight settle more heavily against her as sleep claimed him despite his best efforts to stay awake.

"I think I'll head inside before I fall asleep too," Ruby said.

Chuck stood and stretched. "Cade, would you mind banking the fire when you're through?"

"Of course," Cade replied, settling deeper into his chair as if he had no immediate plans to leave.

As Eva's parents gathered the s'mores supplies and headed toward the house with quiet goodnights, she found herself enjoying the peace and quiet, Noah sleeping peacefully in her arms.

"What happened to Noah's father?"

The question was so unexpected that Eva startled, looking over to find Cade watching her with the careful attention of someone who'd been wondering about this for a while but hadn't found the courage to ask.

Eva shifted slightly in her chair, adjusting Noah's position while she gathered her thoughts. This wasn't a story she often shared, but Cade's genuine interest made her want to be honest about the experience that had shaped both her and her son.

"David had a heart defect that nobody knew about. He collapsed during football practice when I was four months pregnant. The doctors said it was instantaneous—he wouldn't have suffered."

Cade's sharp intake of breath was the only sound for a moment.

"I'm sorry," he said.

"I was twenty-two," Eva continued, finding it easier to tell the story while looking at the fire rather than at Cade's face. "Suddenly a widow and pregnant and terrified. The first few months were... dark. I didn't know how to be pregnant without him there to share it and didn't know how to plan for a baby I'd have to raise alone."

"But you managed."

"Barely." Eva's laugh held no humor. "Mom came and stayed with us for a month after Noah was born. I was so scared of making mistakes, of not being enough for him. Every decision felt enormous because my husband wasn't there to share the responsibility with."

She paused, remembering those overwhelming early days when even simple tasks like grocery shopping had felt insurmountable. "But gradually, I figured it out. Or Noah and I figured it out together. And my faith..." She trailed off, then started again. "My faith was what carried me through. The belief that God had a plan even when I couldn't see it, that David's love was still part of our story even though he couldn't be physically present."

Cade was quiet for a long moment, staring into the fire with an expression Eva couldn't quite read. When he finally spoke, his voice was carefully neutral.

"Do you miss him?"

"I do. I think there will always be a part of me that misses David. He was a good man, and he loved me completely in the time we had together."

She felt Cade's stillness beside her, sensed rather than saw the way he processed her words.

"But missing him doesn't mean I'm not open to new possibilities," she added.

Noah stirred in her arms, mumbling something incoherent against her shoulder. Eva glanced at her watch and sighed.

"I hate to end this," she said, genuine regret in her voice, "but I need to get this little guy home and into bed."

Cade nodded and stood immediately. "Here, let me help."

Without waiting for her agreement, he gently lifted Noah from her arms, the boy's head settling against his shoulder. Cade carried him toward her SUV, while Eva followed.

At the vehicle, Cade settled Noah into his booster seat with surprising gentleness, then stepped back to let Eva handle the complex array of straps and buckles.

"I have no idea how those contraptions work," he admitted.

"It's more complicated than it should be."

Cade walked around to the driver's side and opened her door with old-fashioned courtesy that made her heart flutter. As she was about to climb in, she remembered the fire.

"Don't forget to bank the fire," she said, then paused when she saw him looking off toward the mountains with an expression that seemed almost wistful.

"I think I'll hang out by the fire for a little while longer," he said.

Something about his tone—the loneliness in it—made Eva reach for his hand. His fingers were warm and calloused, and when he looked down at their joined hands, she saw surprise flicker across his features.

"Cade," she said. "You're a good man. You need to start believing that again."

He squeezed her fingers gently, then nodded.

"Goodnight, Eva," he said.

"Goodnight," she said, releasing his hand and climbing into the driver's seat.

As she drove away, Eva watched in her rearview mirror as Cade stood motionless, watching her go. Something about his solitary figure tugged at her heart, reminding her of the day years ago when she had driven away from him headed to college. Her eyes started burning with tears.

"God, I know you have your hands on this situation. Show me what to do," she said as she drove. "Help him, Lord... he really needs you."

Chapter 25

Sunday, June 21st...

Sandpaper against wood provided the perfect soundtrack for a quiet Sunday afternoon as Cade worked on the hope chest. The garage door stood open, allowing the breeze to enter, and country music drifted from his old radio.

He paused to examine his progress, running his fingers along the smooth curves where he'd been working out the final imperfections in the wood grain. Soon it would be ready for a few coats of stain and then the hardware that would transform it from a woodworking project into something beautiful enough to hold someone's most precious treasures.

The sound of an approaching engine made him look up from his work, and his pulse quickened. He set down his sandpaper and walked to the edge of the garage, leaning against the door frame as she parked and climbed out of her vehicle.

Eva was dressed for church in a silky lavender dress that caught the afternoon sunlight and made her skin glow with an ethereal beauty that seemed almost too perfect to be real. The delicate lace details at the neckline and sleeves managed to be both modest and utterly feminine, while her matching Sunday hat enhanced her natural radiance.

"What are you working on today?" she asked.

Cade gestured toward the inside of the garage. "Same thing. Come take a look."

Eva stepped into his workspace. When she saw the hope chest in its current state of near-completion, her intake of breath was audible.

"Cade... I can't believe the talent you have."

"I should be able to start staining it soon," he said, trying not to notice how the garage lighting made her dress shimmer. "So... what are your plans for this afternoon?"

Eva's smile turned slightly mischievous. "You and I are going to paint."

Cade tilted his head and raised an eyebrow. "Paint?"

"Go change into work clothes and come down to the house," she said with the kind of cheerful authority that brooked no argument. "I have a parlor that needs to be painted."

Before Cade could formulate a response, she was pressing an envelope into his hands and walking out of the garage.

"Eva, wait—" he started, but she was already climbing behind the wheel with a wave and a grin that suggested she knew exactly what she was doing.

Cade stood in his driveway watching her taillights, holding the envelope and shaking his head at the woman who seemed determined to dismantle every wall he'd built around his heart.

He opened the envelope and withdrew both a folded note and a photograph that made him pause. The image showed two teenagers sitting on a scaffold twenty feet in the air, their backs to the camera as they applied fresh white paint to the side of a barn. Even from behind, he recognized himself and Eva. They were seventeen years old then.

The memory hit him with startling clarity—that had been one of the smaller barns on his family's ranch, completed just a week before this photo was taken. His father had hired a company to build it, but Cade had volunteered to handle the painting himself. Eva had shown up that morning with paintbrushes and the kind of cheerful determination that made even tedious jobs feel like adventures.

Cade could still remember the exact moment when he'd set down his paintbrush and looked at her.

"I think I'm falling in love with you," he'd said.

Eva had looked at him with those blue eyes that always seemed to see straight through to his soul, and her smile had been radiant. "I already know I love you," she'd replied with the kind of honest certainty that had characterized everything about her.

Their first kiss had happened twenty feet in the air on a painter's scaffold.

Cade grinned at the memory as he unfolded her note:

"He heals the brokenhearted and binds up their wounds." – Psalm 147:3

You once reminded me I was more than my mistakes. Let me return the favor. Some wounds don't scar—they bloom into testimony. (Now, go change and come down to the house!)

The symbolism wasn't lost on him—painting was about renewal, about covering the old with something fresh and beautiful.

Cade looked at the photograph one more time, remembering what it had felt like to be certain about love, to believe in futures that stretched out like uncharted territory full of possibility.

Laughing at his own surrender to the inevitable, Cade headed inside his cabin to change into work clothes.

Chapter 26

Eva pushed the porch swing gently with her feet as she watched for Cade's truck to appear around the bend. She'd changed from her church dress into her most comfortable painting clothes—faded jeans with holes in both knees and an oversized t-shirt that had seen better days. Her hair was pulled back in a simple clip, and she'd already scrubbed off every trace of makeup, preparing for an afternoon of serious work.

When Cade's red pickup finally came into view, Eva felt that familiar flutter in her chest that had been growing stronger each day. He parked in front of the bed and breakfast and climbed out wearing old jeans, a faded t-shirt, and boots that had seen plenty of honest labor.

"Where did you get that picture?" he asked without preamble as he approached the porch.

Eva smiled. "Your mom gave it to me not long after she took it."

Cade's expression softened at the mention of his mother, and Eva caught a glimpse of the grief that still lived in his eyes when he thought about the parents he'd lost too young.

"It's quiet," he observed, glancing around.

"Noah's with Mom and Dad," Eva explained, standing and smoothing down her t-shirt. "They took him for ice cream after church, and then they were heading to the park. He'll be thoroughly spoiled by the time they bring him home. Come on in," she said.

Cade followed her through the front door, and Eva noticed the way his gaze took in the changes she'd made over the past week. The foyer had been painted a warm cream color that complemented the stained glass window perfectly, while the hallway leading to the kitchen was now free of the dated wallpaper that had made the space feel closed in.

"You've been busy," he said with obvious approval.

"We'll tackle the parlor today," Eva replied, guiding him into the space that would serve as a comfortable gathering area for her future guests.

Everything was ready for their painting project—drop cloths covered the furniture, blue painter's tape protected the trim and window edges, and two gallons of a soft, warm butter yellow paint sat waiting beside rollers, brushes, and trays.

He moved immediately to one of the paint cans, prying open the lid. "So how long are your notes going to keep appearing?"

"That's not for you to worry about," she replied with deliberate cheerfulness.

Cade looked up at her then, and Eva saw the questions in his eyes.

"You know exactly what you're doing, don't you?" he said quietly.

Eva grinned, abandoning any pretense of innocence. "Of course I do. Is it working?"

Cade poured paint into each of the trays. "That's not for you to worry about, Eva Blankenship," he said, grabbing both rollers and handing her one with something that looked suspiciously like a smile tugging at his lips.

They each claimed a ladder and began the methodical work of covering the walls with fresh paint.

"What do you remember about that day?" she asked eventually. "The day from the picture I gave you earlier."

Cade paused in his painting, his roller suspended halfway down the wall. "Which part?"

Eva stopped painting entirely and turned to face him, waiting until he looked her way before speaking. "You told me, 'I think I'm falling in love with you.' I told you I already loved you. And you know something, Cade? I still do. That's never changed. I'll always carry a piece of you in my heart."

The silence that followed was so complete that Eva could hear her heartbeat. Cade's face went blank, and he turned back to his painting with movements that seemed forced rather than natural.

Eva didn't resume her work. Instead, she continued to watch him, noting the tension in his shoulders and the way his jaw had tightened at her declaration.

"You're staring," he said without turning around.

She didn't deny it and didn't look away.

Finally, Cade set down his roller and looked at her with something that might have been desperation. "You're driving me mad," he said, his voice rough with emotion he couldn't hide.

"Good," Eva replied, feeling a surge of triumph at getting such an honest reaction from him. "I'm glad I haven't lost my touch."

They returned to painting, but the atmosphere had shifted, becoming charged with the kind of sparks that made everything they did or said feel significant. Eva waited until they'd finished most of one wall before asking the question that had been building in her mind for days.

"Tell me about Rachel," she said, dipping her roller in fresh paint with studied casualness.

Cade's hand stilled completely. "Eva—"

"Don't avoid the subject," she interrupted firmly. "Tell me about her. How you met, what she was like, and what happened."

For a moment, Eva thought he might refuse.

"I met her at a cattle auction in Billings," Cade said finally. "She was there with her father, who was looking to buy some breeding stock. She seemed... interested in ranch life. Asked questions about the cattle and my ranch, said she'd always dreamed of living in the country."

Eva kept painting, giving him the space to tell his story without feeling pressured or watched.

"She was beautiful," Cade continued. "Sophisticated in ways that made me feel like maybe I was more than just a small-town rancher. When she agreed to go to dinner with me, I couldn't believe someone like her would be interested in someone like me."

"Six months from that first dinner to our wedding," Cade said, moving his ladder to start on the next section of wall. "She seemed to love everything about ranch life in the country and the quiet lifestyle. Said it was exactly what she'd been looking for."

"But it wasn't?"

Cade's laugh held no humor. "The first few months were good. Or I thought so at the time. Looking back now, there were signs she was getting restless. Something in her changed. She was showing a side of her I hadn't seen before."

He paused in his painting, staring at the wall as if he could see his past there.

"Then she was spending more time in Billings. Shopping trips that lasted longer than they should have, overnight and weekend trips. Extended visits with friends I'd never met. She started talking about how isolated the ranch was and how limited our social opportunities were."

Eva felt her chest tighten with anger at the woman who'd systematically dismantled this good man's confidence, but she kept her expression neutral.

" A year into our marriage, and she wanted me to sell the ranch," Cade continued, his voice growing rougher. "Said my skills could translate to agricultural consulting, that I could make more money in the city. When I refused..." He trailed off, shaking his head.

"When you refused, what happened?"

"She found someone else," Cade said simply. "A lawyer she met during one of her shopping trips."

"She had an affair."

"For months, and I had no idea it was going on," Cade confirmed. "The worst part wasn't even the betrayal, though that nearly killed me. It was how calculated everything was. This lawyer—the man she's married to now—structured the divorce settlement to cause maximum damage."

"She destroyed your family's legacy," Eva said, the words barely above a whisper.

"Three generations of Mayer family history, gone in one legal document," Cade said, and Eva heard the old pain still raw in his voice. "And sadly... I question to this day if she had a plan all along. Did she ever love me? Did she target me from day one looking for a payout to support her lifestyle?"

Eva felt something fierce and protective rise in her chest. She set down her paint roller in the tray attached to her ladder and climbed down with deliberate purpose.

Cade watched her, confusion flickering across his features.

"Come down here," she said, her voice gentle but commanding.

He descended from his ladder slowly, wariness in every movement, as if he wasn't sure what to expect from her. The moment he turned to face her, Eva stepped forward and wrapped her arms around him in a bear hug so fierce and unexpected that it knocked him back a step.

"What's this for?" he asked, his voice muffled against her hair. His arms had come up instinctively to hold her.

Eva rested her head against his chest, listening to the rapid rhythm beneath her ear. "Do you feel that?" she asked softly.

"What... you squeezing me to death?" he replied, though she could hear the hint of laughter in his voice.

"No," Eva said, pulling back just enough to look up at him without letting go. "Your heart is beating a hundred miles a minute. And you know what that tells me?"

Cade looked down at her. "That I'm alive?"

"Well, yeah, that," Eva said with a soft laugh. "And that you survived a marriage gone wrong. You survived a divorce that was designed to destroy you. You survived losing your ranch that meant everything to you." Her voice grew stronger, more certain. "And you're still here, Cade. Still standing, still breathing, still capable of letting someone close enough to hear your heartbeat."

She watched as his expression changed, and he glanced away.

"You'll never forget what happened to you," Eva continued. "But don't let it define you. Don't let Rachel's betrayal determine what you're worth or what you deserve."

He looked back down at her with an intensity that made the air between them feel charged with electricity. Eva could see the moment when Cade's defenses crumbled. She stretched up on her tiptoes, drawn by something stronger than caution or common sense, close enough that she could feel his breath on her face.

Just as Cade began to lower his head toward hers, the front door burst open with the sound of excited voices and hurried footsteps.

"Mom! We're back!"

Noah stopped short when he saw them, tilting his head with the curious expression of a child trying to process what he was witnessing. Behind him, Ruby and Chuck appeared, taking in the scene with varying degrees of amusement.

"Well," Ruby said with a smile, "what kind of painting party did we walk into?"

Eva stepped back from Cade, her cheeks flushing as she tried to look like she hadn't just been about to kiss him senseless in the middle of her parlor. Cade cleared his throat and ran a hand through his hair, looking adorably flustered in a way that made Eva's heart race all over again.

"Just... working on the walls," Eva managed, gesturing vaguely at their paint-covered surroundings.

"Uh-huh," Ruby said with the knowing smile of a mother who could read between every line. "And how's that working out for you?"

"Oh... you know... not bad... not too bad at all."

Chapter 27

Ruby's gentle laughter filled the awkward silence. "Well, I think your dad and I should take Noah back to the ranch and let you two finish this painting project properly."

Eva felt heat rise in her cheeks as she stared at the half-finished wall as if it held the secrets of the universe.

"What do you say, partner?" Chuck's voice boomed with grandfatherly enthusiasm as he turned to Noah. "Want to come help with afternoon chores? Those horses and cattle won't feed themselves."

Noah's face lit up like Christmas morning. "Really? Even the important stuff?"

"Especially the important stuff," Chuck confirmed with a wink. "Cowboys always take care of their animals first."

Ruby was already heading toward the staircase with purposeful steps. "Let me grab some play clothes for you, sweetheart. Can't have you doing ranch work in your Sunday best."

As Ruby disappeared up the stairs, a silence settled over the remaining adults. Eva watched as Cade ran a hand through his hair again, his expression a mixture of embarrassment and something that looked almost like panic.

"Chuck, I'm sorry about—" Cade began, but Ruby's voice cut through his words from the second floor.

"No apologies, Cade," she called out firmly. "Don't make excuses for being human."

Chuck nodded approvingly at his wife's wisdom. "She's right, you know. Nothing wrong with two people remembering what it feels like to care about each other."

Ruby reappeared moments later with a bundle of clothes. "These should do nicely."

Noah accepted the clothes with eager hands, already chattering about everything he hoped to accomplish during the afternoon. "Can I brush Storm? And help with the hay? Check the water troughs?"

"All of that and more," Chuck promised, his eyes twinkling.

Eva hugged her parents. "Thank you," she whispered, knowing they understood she was grateful for far more than just babysitting.

"Have a good afternoon, you two," Ruby said meaningfully, kissing Eva's cheek before heading toward the front door with Chuck and Noah trailing behind.

The house felt enormous and quiet after their departure, with only the sound of the grandfather clock in the hallway marking the passage of time. Eva stood in the parlor doorway, watching Cade study the paint-spattered drop cloths as if they contained instructions for navigating the emotional minefield they'd just created.

"You know what?" Eva said suddenly. "We're done painting for the day. It's Sunday—let's just enjoy the afternoon on the front porch."

Without waiting for his response, she turned and headed toward the kitchen. The refrigerator held a pitcher of fresh lemonade she'd made that morning, and the cookie jar contained a batch of snickerdoodles she'd made earlier in the week. Simple pleasures, but sometimes simple was exactly what a complicated situation needed.

Eva gathered glasses and arranged everything on a tray, her movements automatic as her mind processed the magnitude of what had just happened.

"Come on," she said as she passed the parlor where Cade still stood, his hands shoved deep in his pockets and his expression unreadable.

The front porch welcomed them with its promise of peaceful conversation and mountain views that put human problems into perspective. Eva set the tray on the small table and poured glasses of lemonade, then settled onto the porch swing.

Cade joined her after a moment's hesitation, accepting the glass of lemonade she offered. They sat in silence, the swing creaking softly as it moved back and forth.

Eva studied Cade's profile as he gazed out at the rolling pastures that stretched toward the mountains. The strong line of his jaw, the way his dark hair caught the light, the careful distance he maintained even while sitting close enough to touch—everything about him spoke of a man who'd learned to protect himself by expecting nothing good to last.

"You know what helped me most about a year after David died?" Eva said finally, setting down her glass and turning to face him more fully. "I realized I was living in a rut. I was stuck in this deep, dark hole and couldn't see my way out of it."

"I did a lot of soul-searching," Eva continued, her voice soft but steady. "I realized I couldn't move forward until I made some changes. I was angry at God for letting David die so young. I was angry at David for leaving me to raise Noah alone. I was angry at myself for not being there that day he died on the football field, for not somehow preventing what happened."

The swing slowed to a stop as Eva set her feet firmly on the porch floor. She reached over and took the glass from Cade's hands, setting it aside before turning to face him completely. When he still wouldn't meet her eyes, she cupped his face in her hands, her palms warm against his skin.

"Forgive yourself, Cade," she whispered, her voice thick with emotion. "Forgive yourself. What you went through—yes, I'm sure it was devastating. Yes, it hurt more than anyone should have to bear. But it's over, and it's done with. Let that anger go."

Cade's green eyes finally met hers, and Eva saw pain so deep it made her chest hurt. "God's got this," she continued, her thumbs stroking gently across his cheekbones. "And even though this might sound cliché and too simple, listen to me—let it go and give it to God."

Cade's hands came up to cover hers, his touch careful and reverent. "That all sounds easy," he said, his voice rough. "But it's easier said than done, Eva. I had my world ripped out from underneath me. Losing the ranch made me feel like less of a man. How do you come back from something like that? Here I am, thirty years old, and all I have to my name is my truck, a horse, and a few belongings. I have nothing."

Eva's hands tightened on his face, her eyes blazing with fierce conviction. "You're so wrong. You think your worth is measured by what you own? By some piece of paper that says you have a deed to land?" She leaned closer, her forehead almost touching his. "You have integrity, Cade. You have skills and knowledge and a work ethic that any employer would value. You have hands that can fix anything broken and a heart that's capable of such deep love it scares you to death. You think those things don't matter? You think they're not enough?"

Cade's eyes closed, and Eva saw the internal battle playing out across his features.

"Rachel was selfish and cruel. She took advantage of your generous heart and your willingness to trust. That says everything about her character and nothing about yours."

Eva shifted, never breaking the intimate contact between them. "You want to know what I see when I look at you? I see a man who's been beaten down but not broken. I see someone who still shows up for work every day, who still treats people with kindness, who still has room in his heart to care about a little boy, and a man who still loves and respects my parents."

Cade's hands dropped from hers, but Eva didn't let go of his face. "I see the man I fell in love with when I was seventeen, and I see the man I could love even more deeply now because I understand what real hardship and real loss can teach us about what matters most."

"Eva—" Cade started, but she shook her head.

"You cannot continue living like this, Cade. Shutting yourself off from the world will eventually lead you deeper into a long and lonely life. God gave you one life to live—don't waste it hiding from the possibility of joy because you're afraid of being hurt again."

The afternoon air was warm and still around them, filled with the scent of wildflowers and the distant sound of cattle lowing in the pastures. Eva could hear the grandfather clock chiming the hour inside the house, marking time that seemed both precious and fleeting.

"Maybe," she said carefully, "you should talk to Pastor Sam. He's helped a lot of people work through difficult times. He might be able to help you find a new path, a new direction, or just a new way of thinking about where you are right now."

Cade was quiet for a long moment. "I don't know if I remember how to have faith," he said finally. "I don't know if I remember how to trust that good things can happen."

"Then start small," Eva suggested gently. "Trust that this moment is good. Trust that Noah's laughter when he sees you is real. Trust that my parents genuinely care about you, and that maybe—just maybe—you deserve to be happy."

She released his face and took his hands in hers, marveling at the contrast between his calloused palms and her softer fingers. "Faith isn't about having all the answers, Cade. It's about taking the next step even when you can't see the whole road ahead."

She shifted and sat back in the porch swing and continued its gentle motion as they sat holding hands. Eva glanced at him, watching the play of emotions across his face—hope warring with fear, longing battling with self-protection, and the gradual softening of features that had been held rigid for too long.

"I've been so angry," he admitted quietly. "At Rachel, at God, at myself. At the whole world for not being fair. I don't know how to let that go."

"One day at a time," Eva said simply. "One choice at a time. Choose to forgive yourself for trusting the wrong person. Choose to believe that your worth isn't determined by what you lost. Choose to let people who care about you back into your life... completely."

The sound of laughter drifted across the distance from the direction of the ranch, where Noah was probably having the time of his life helping with chores and learning everything he could about ranch life. Eva smiled at the thought of her son's boundless enthusiasm and the way Cade's face lit up whenever Noah directed his endless questions toward him.

"That boy thinks you hung the moon," she said. "He needs what you have to offer, Cade. Your knowledge, your patience, your example of what a good man looks like. Don't let your fear of being hurt again rob him of that."

Cade squeezed her hand, his grip warm and strong. "I don't want to let him down. I don't want to be that person who disappoints him."

"Then don't be," Eva said with gentle firmness. "Be the man I know you are. Be the man you were before someone tried to convince you that you weren't enough."

She stood, never letting his hand go. "Enough of all this serious talk," she said with a smile that was both gentle and determined. "I think I've given you enough to think about for one afternoon. Let's go enjoy our day."

Cade looked up at her, his expression a mixture of gratitude and something that might have been the beginning of hope. "What did you have in mind?"

Eva tugged gently on his hand, encouraging him to stand. "I know a little boy that would be happy if you went and helped with those ranch chores. What do you say?"

For a moment, Cade hesitated, and Eva could see the internal struggle playing out in his eyes. Then, slowly, he nodded and allowed her to pull him to his feet. His hand was warm in hers, steady and real, and Eva felt a flutter of hope.

Chapter 28

Storm's hooves drummed a steady rhythm against the packed earth as they approached the cabin, both horse and rider grateful for the respite from the morning's work. Cade had spent the better part of four hours this morning in the saddle under a sun that seemed determined to remind everyone that summer in Montana could be every bit as punishing as winter. The prospect of a cool drink and a quiet lunch in his own space had grown increasingly appealing as the morning wore on.

The decision to skip lunch with the ranch hands in the bunkhouse had been spontaneous, born from a need for solitude that had nothing to do with the quality of company and everything to do with the restless energy that had been building in his chest since yesterday's conversation with Eva on her front porch. Her words had lodged themselves somewhere deep in his mind, creating an uncomfortable itch that no amount of hard work seemed able to scratch.

Forgive yourself, Cade.

The memory of her voice, soft but certain, made his hands tighten slightly on Storm's reins. How did a man forgive himself for being so spectacularly wrong about someone? How did he reconcile the devastating betrayal that had cost him everything with Eva's gentle insistence that his worth wasn't measured by what he'd lost?

As the cabin came into view, nestled among the cottonwood trees that provided blessed shade during the heat of summer days, Cade's attention was immediately drawn to the familiar white rectangle tucked between his screen door and the doorframe.

Nine days.

Nine consecutive days of Eva's persistent kindness, and the sight of that envelope brought a smile to his lips.

He dismounted with the fluid grace of someone who'd been climbing off horses since before he could properly tie his shoes, his boots hitting the ground with a soft thud that sent a nearby meadowlark into flight. Storm snorted softly and shook his head, clearly ready for his own midday rest in the shade of the trees.

"Go on," Cade said, giving the horse's neck an affectionate pat. "Find yourself some shade. You've earned it."

Storm needed no further encouragement, ambling toward the tree-line with the unhurried confidence of an animal who knew exactly where the best grass could be found. Cade watched him go for a moment, then turned his attention to the envelope that seemed to beckon from his front door like a small flag of hope.

He climbed the steps in two long strides, pulled the envelope free, and entered the cabin. The interior was cool and dim after the blazing sunshine, and Cade took a moment to let his eyes adjust.

He set the envelope on the dining table next to the wooden box.

Lunch first, he decided with the practical mind of a man who'd learned that physical needs required attention before emotional ones could be addressed. The refrigerator yielded the makings of a respectable Italian sub—salami, provolone, tomatoes, and lettuce crisp enough to provide a satisfying crunch. He added a thin layer of mustard and a drizzle of olive oil, creating the kind of simple meal that could fuel a man through the afternoon's work without weighing him down.

Settling into his usual chair at the table, Cade took a substantial bite of the sandwich and allowed himself to savor both the flavors and the blessed quiet of his home. Through the kitchen window, he could see Storm rolling in the grass with the kind of undignified pleasure that always made Cade shake his head in amusement. Some things never changed, and there was comfort in that consistency.

After another bite of sandwich, Cade's curiosity finally overcame his tendency to postpone emotional challenges until they could no longer be avoided. He tore open the envelope and unfolded the paper inside:

"There is therefore now no condemnation for those who are in Christ Jesus." – Romans 8:1

That voice telling you you're not enough? It's lying.

Cade stared at the words until they blurred slightly, his throat tightening with an emotion he couldn't quite name. She knew. Somehow, Eva had looked straight through all his carefully constructed defenses and seen the core wound that had been festering since the day Rachel walked out of his life—the insidious voice that whispered he would never be enough.

Not enough to keep a wife satisfied. Not enough to deserve the kind of love that stayed when things got difficult. Not enough to risk his heart on the possibility that someone might choose him and mean it.

He folded the note and opened the wooden box, adding Eva's latest message to the growing collection that had become more precious to him than any treasure he could imagine. But instead of closing the lid, he reached for the two photographs that lay inside.

He set both pictures in front of him on the table and took another bite of his sandwich, though it might as well have been sawdust for all the attention he paid to the taste. His mind was too occupied with memories of what was and painful speculation about what might have been if they'd made different choices during that last week before she left for college.

The breakup had been mutual, technically. Both of them had recognized the practical impossibility of maintaining a long-distance relationship when Eva was destined for bigger things than Riverbend Valley could offer and he was rooted to the land with every fiber of his being. They'd been mature about it, civilized.

But what if they'd been wrong? What if love had been enough, and they'd simply been too young and too scared to fight for what they had?

The thoughts that followed were dangerous territory, the kind of speculation that could drive a man mad with regret and impossible wishes. If he'd asked her to stay, would she have chosen him over college? If he'd been willing to leave the ranch and follow her into whatever life she wanted to build, would they have found a way to make it work?

Would they have been the kind of couple who grew old together, who weathered storms and celebrated victories as a team? Would there have been children with Eva's blue eyes and his stubbornness, little ones who learned to ride horses before they could properly tie their shoes?

Cade closed his eyes and let his head fall back against the chair, overwhelmed by the questions that had no answers and possibilities that belonged to the realm of dreams rather than reality. The practical part of his mind reminded him that this kind of thinking was not only pointless but dangerous—dwelling on alternate histories was a luxury he couldn't afford when the present demanded all his attention and energy.

But Eva's daily messages had been systematically weakening his defenses against hope, and hope was perhaps the most dangerous emotion of all. Hope made a man vulnerable to disappointment, made him believe in possibilities that might prove to be nothing more than cruel illusions.

That voice telling you you're not enough? It's lying.

Cade opened his eyes and looked again at the graduation photograph, studying the face of the eighteen-year-old boy who'd believed anything he dreamed of was possible.

Maybe it was time to remember what it felt like to be that boy again.

Chapter 29

*T*uesday, June 23rd...

Storm's breathing was as labored as Cade's own as they approached the cabin, both of them ready for the blessed relief of shade and rest after a morning that had tested every ounce of their endurance. The heat had been relentless. The kind that shimmered off the ground in waves and made even the simplest tasks feel like monumental efforts, but it was more than physical exhaustion weighing on Cade's shoulders as he dismounted.

Ten days.

Ten days of Eva's daily messages.

Ten days of scripture verses and gentle encouragement.

The constant swirl of thoughts rolling around in his mind had left him feeling more drained than any amount of physical labor ever could.

The white envelope tucked between his screen door and the door-frame had become as reliable as sunrise. Each message seemed to cut a little deeper than the last, reaching into places he'd thought were safely buried.

Inside the cabin, the temperature was only marginally cooler, but the absence of direct sunlight felt perfect. Cade dropped the envelope on the dining table and headed straight for the kitchen, his body moving on autopilot.

The refrigerator revealed milk, and the pantry yielded a box of cornflakes that would require minimal effort to eat—exactly what his current state of mental exhaustion demanded.

Settling into his chair at the table, he poured milk over the golden flakes and took his first spoonful before reaching for the envelope that seemed to pulse with promise.

"The old has gone, the new is here." – 2 Corinthians 5:17

Today she was reminding him that the past didn't have to define his future.

The old has gone, the new is here.

Cade stared at the words until they blurred, his spoon suspended halfway between bowl and mouth as the full implications of the verse settled over him.

He folded the note and added it to the wooden box as he got up from the table.

The bookshelf in his living room held assorted books—agricultural manuals, a few paperback novels, and, tucked between a veterinary guide and a collection of Western short stories, the leather-bound Bible his mother had given him on his eighteenth birthday. The cover was worn smooth from years of handling.

Cade pulled the Bible from its resting place and returned to the dining table. He opened to 2 Corinthians 5, his fingers remembering the texture of pages he'd once turned regularly.

"Therefore, if anyone is in Christ, the new creation has come: The old has gone, the new is here!"

The exclamation point at the end of the verse seemed to leap off the page, a celebration of possibility that made his chest tighten with hope. He read the surrounding verses, letting the familiar language wash over him like water on parched ground, remembering what it had felt like to believe in divine love and perfect timing and the promise that all things could work together for good.

Had it really been so long since he'd opened this book? Since he'd sought comfort in words that had once been as much a part of his daily routine as morning coffee and afternoon chores?

The cereal grew soggy as he read, but Cade found himself unable to stop turning pages, drawn deeper into passages that spoke of redemption and renewal.

His mother had marked verses in blue ink, her careful handwriting noting dates and circumstances that had made certain passages particularly meaningful to her.

"For our light and momentary troubles are achieving for us an eternal glory that far outweighs them all," read one notation from 2 Corinthians 4:17.

Below it, in his father's shakier script:

"Trust in His timing, son. Always trust in His timing."

The words blurred as tears gathered in his eyes.

The cereal sat forgotten as he continued reading, his soul drinking in words of hope like a man dying of thirst. Outside, Storm grazed contentedly in the shade, while inside his master slowly remembered what it felt like to hope for more than mere survival.

The old has gone, the new is here.

Chapter 30

The late afternoon sun painted everything in shades of gold as Eva adjusted the stirrups on Daisy's saddle, the gentle pony standing with the patience of a saint while Noah bounced on his toes beside her. They'd been working in the smaller corral for the better part of an hour, and Eva could see the confidence building in her son's posture with each successful mount and dismount.

"Remember what Grandpa taught you," Eva said, holding the pony's bridle while Noah prepared to swing up into the saddle. "Smooth movements, keep your voice calm, and always let Daisy know where you are."

"I know, Mom," Noah said with the long-suffering patience of an eight-year-old who'd heard the same instructions multiple times.

Eva smiled at his determination, watching as he placed his left foot in the stirrup and pulled himself up. Daisy didn't so much as twitch, her brown eyes half-closed.

The sound of hoofbeats approaching made Eva look up. Cade was riding toward the barn complex on Storm, both of them dust-covered and showing signs of a long afternoon in the summer heat. Even from a distance, she could see the way he sat in the saddle with unconscious grace, moving with his horse in perfect harmony.

As he drew closer, Cade's attention focused on the scene before him.

"Cade!" Noah called out, waving enthusiastically from Daisy's back. "Look! I'm riding all by myself!"

Cade dismounted and tethered Storm to the corral fence, then climbed up. He settled on the top rail as he watched Noah guide Daisy in a careful circle around the corral.

"That's some fine riding," Cade said. "Daisy looks like she's enjoying having a real cowboy in the saddle."

Noah's face lit up and his shoulders straightened with pride. "I've been practicing."

"Why don't you come join us?" Eva said.

"Please, Cade?"

The combination of Noah's eager plea and Eva's invitation had Cade jumping down from the fence rail.

"Show me how you hold your reins, partner," he said.

Noah demonstrated his grip, and Eva watched as Cade made minor adjustments to the boy's hand position with gentle precision. There was something almost reverent about the way he touched Noah's small fingers, guiding them into the proper placement with the care of someone handling something precious and fragile.

"That's better," Cade said. "Now, when you want Daisy to turn, you don't pull on her mouth. You use neck reining—remember me showing you this?" He demonstrated the subtle movement with his hands, then guided Noah through the motion.

Eva moved to lean against the fence, content to watch as Cade took over the lesson. She'd seen him interact with Noah many times over the past weeks, but there was something different about today—a genuine smile that reached his eyes.

"Can I trot now?" Noah asked after successfully demonstrating several turns and stops.

Cade glanced at Eva, seeking permission with raised eyebrows. When she nodded, he turned back to Noah with serious attention.

"Trotting is different from walking," Cade explained, moving to walk beside Daisy as they began to move. "You're going to want to bounce at first, but the secret is to move with the horse, not against her."

Eva watched as Noah concentrated with fierce determination, his small body adjusting to Daisy's gait under Cade's patient guidance. The pony was the perfect teacher—steady, predictable, and forgiving of the inevitable wobbles and corrections that came with learning.

"I'm doing it!" Noah exclaimed as he found his rhythm, his face glowing with accomplishment. "Look, Mom! I'm trotting!"

"I can see that, sweetheart," Eva called back, her voice thick with maternal pride. "You're doing great."

But her attention was as much on Cade as it was on Noah. She could see the transformation happening in real time—the way his shoulders had lost their defensive hunch, the genuine laughter that escaped when Noah made a particularly enthusiastic observation about Daisy's personality and the unconscious protectiveness in the way he positioned himself to catch the boy if he should lose his balance.

"Think you're ready for a little adventure?" Cade asked Noah after several successful circuits of the corral. "There's a nice flat stretch of pasture right behind the barn that's perfect for practicing in a bigger space."

Noah's eyes widened with excitement. "Really? I can ride in a real pasture?"

"With both of us right there with you," Cade assured him. "What do you say, Mom? Ready to let this cowboy spread his wings a little?"

"I think that sounds perfect."

The next hour passed in a golden haze of summer afternoon magic. Noah rode Daisy around the pasture with Eva and Cade walking or jogging on either side, his confidence growing with each step. They talked about everything and nothing.

Later, as they made their way back toward the barn, Eva found herself falling back slightly to watch Cade and her son. Cade's hand rested lightly on Daisy's, ready to steady Noah if needed, while he listened with complete attention to the boy's rapid-fire dialogue.

Eva felt her chest tighten with emotion so intense it was almost painful. This was what she'd dreamed of without quite realizing it—not just Noah learning to ride, but Noah having a man in his life who cared about his progress, who took time to teach him properly, who saw his potential and nurtured it with patient hands and encouraging words.

As they reached the barn and began the process of unsaddling Daisy and settling her for the evening, Eva stepped back to lean against the fence and simply watch. Noah was explaining to Cade why he thought Daisy was the smartest pony in the world, while Cade nodded seriously and asked thoughtful questions that made the boy feel heard and valued.

The sun was beginning to set behind the mountains, painting the sky in brilliant shades of orange and pink that reflected off the ranch buildings. The scene before her was so perfect, so exactly what she'd hoped for, that Eva felt tears prick at the corners of her eyes.

She tilted her face toward the heavens and let her heart speak the words that had been building all afternoon.

Thank you, she thought, the prayer rising from the deepest part of her soul. *Thank you for bringing us home. Thank you for second chances and patient hearts and little boys who see the best in everyone. Thank you for whatever you're doing in Cade's heart, for the man he's becoming again, and for the way he looks at Noah like he's precious and worthy of care.*

Eva closed her eyes and let the peace of the moment settle over her like a blessing, knowing with absolute certainty that God had his hand on everything.

When she opened her eyes, Cade was looking at her with an expression that made her breath catch. There was tenderness there and gratitude.

Thank you, Eva repeated silently, watching as Noah threw his arms around Cade's waist in an impulsive hug that the man returned without hesitation.

Thank you for all of it.

Chapter 31

Wednesday, June 24th...

The Black Angus cattle grazed contentedly in the morning sunshine, their dark coats gleaming as they moved slowly across the pasture toward the creek. Cade adjusted his position in the saddle and squinted against the bright sun, mentally counting heads while Storm shifted beneath him with the patience of a horse accustomed to long stretches of watching and waiting.

"I'm thinking we could handle another forty head," Chuck said, leaning forward to rest his forearms on his saddle horn. "This grass is some of the best we've had in years, and the water supply's been consistent."

"Market prices are solid too," Cade agreed, his gaze sweeping across the rolling pasture that stretched toward the distant mountains. "We'd need to upgrade the handling facilities in the north pasture, but that's manageable."

Chuck nodded approvingly. "Well, look who's coming," he said, as his attention shifted to the east.

Cade turned to follow Chuck's gaze and felt his pulse quicken at the sight of Eva approaching on Buttercup, with Noah seated in front of her.

As they drew closer, Noah's excited voice carried across the pasture. "Grandpa! Cade! We came to find you!"

"So I see," Chuck called back with grandfatherly pleasure. "What brings you two out to the back forty this morning?"

Eva guided Buttercup to a stop beside their horses, her smile bright despite the slight shadows under her eyes that spoke of early mornings and late nights.

"Good mornin', Daddy. Cade," she said. "I just needed a ride this morning. The bed and breakfast work is getting a bit overwhelming, and I decided I needed a little fresh air."

Cade noted the way she said it—not complaining, just stating a simple fact. Eva had always been one to push through challenges without making a big production of the difficulties, but he could see the weariness around her eyes that suggested she'd been working too hard.

"Fresh air's good medicine," Chuck agreed. "Nothing like a morning ride to clear the head."

Eva reached into her jeans pocket and withdrew a folded piece of paper, extending it toward Cade.

"Switching up your delivery methods, I see," he said, accepting the note with a grin.

"Variety is the spice of life," Eva replied with a laugh. "You boys enjoy yourselves. Noah and I are going for a ride."

But Noah had other ideas. He twisted in the saddle to look back at his mother with hopeful blue eyes. "Can I stay here with Grandpa and Cade? Please?"

Eva hesitated for just a moment, then nodded. "Which horse do you want to ride?"

"Cade's," Noah answered without hesitation.

Eva guided Buttercup closer to Storm, and Cade reached over to lift Noah from his mother's saddle to his own, settling the boy securely in front of him.

"Have a good ride, sweetheart," Chuck said to his daughter.

Eva smiled and nudged Buttercup into motion, taking off at a swift pace that spoke of someone eager to feel the wind in her hair and the freedom of open country beneath her horse's hooves. They watched her go, her figure gradually growing smaller as she headed west.

Chuck chuckled softly. "That girl's always needed space to think when life gets complicated."

Cade nodded, remembering afternoons from their teenage years when Eva would disappear for hours on solitary rides, returning refreshed and ready to tackle whatever challenges awaited her. Some things never changed, and there was comfort in that consistency.

"Can we go check on the cattle up close?" Noah asked, his small hands gripping the saddle horn with excitement.

"In a minute, partner," Cade said, unfolding Eva's note. "Let's see what your mom brought me today."

He read the verse aloud, his voice carrying across the quiet pasture: "'The Lord your God... will take great delight in you... He will rejoice over you with singing.' Zephaniah 3:17."

Chuck was quiet for a long moment, his weathered face thoughtful as he gazed out over the cattle and rolling grassland. When he finally spoke, his voice held the kind of quiet conviction that came from a lifetime of faith tested by both hardship and blessing.

"That girl of mine," he said with a slow shake of his head, "she's got a gift for knowing exactly what a person needs to hear."

Chapter 32

Thursday, June 25th...

The rhythmic scrape of the muck rake against the stall floor provided a steady counterpoint to the conversation as Cade mucked out Storm's stall. Across the barn aisle, Chuck worked with the same methodical efficiency, both men comfortable with the kind of labor that left plenty of room for talking.

"So the Riverbend Rodeo's this Saturday," Chuck said, pausing to lean on his muckrake handle. "You planning on going?"

Cade dumped another forkful of soiled bedding into the wheelbarrow. "Thinking about it."

Chuck gave him a long look that held the patient wisdom of a man who'd spent decades reading between the lines of what people said versus what they meant. "Well, think on it a little harder. I have a daughter and grandson that I'm sure would enjoy going with you."

Cade's hands still on the rake handle. "I have been."

"Mornin', you two."

Cade looked up to see Eva standing in the barn aisle, the morning sunlight behind her creating a halo effect around her. She wore jeans and a light blue blouse, and her smile was bright enough to make his heart beat faster.

"Mornin', sweetheart," Chuck replied, his face lighting up at the sight of his daughter. "What brings you down to the barn this morning?"

Eva approached Cade's stall and handed him a folded piece of paper. "Just making my rounds," she said with a grin that made Cade's pulse quicken.

He accepted the note, unable to suppress his smile.

Chuck chuckled and shook his head. "Is this going to be a daily habit? You interrupting our chores?"

"Possibly," Eva replied without a trace of embarrassment. "I sure hope I'm not bothering you boys."

"You're never a bother," Chuck said firmly, his voice carrying the absolute certainty of paternal love. "Don't you ever think otherwise."

"I've got to run to town for supplies. Do you need anything while I'm out?"

"Can't think of anything," Chuck said. "We're pretty well stocked."

"Noah's up at the house with Mom fixing lunch," Eva continued. "She said to tell you two to come up in about fifteen minutes to eat." She paused and looked directly at Cade. "I'm sure Noah would like to help you with cowboy stuff after lunch, if you don't mind."

The casual way she included him in Noah's afternoon plans sent warmth spreading through his chest.

"Sounds good to me. Your dad and I are going to check the water lines in the pastures... make sure all the tanks are filling okay."

"Perfect." Eva's smile was radiant. "I'll see you both later."

They watched her walk back toward the barn entrance, her stride confident and purposeful. Chuck waited until she was out of earshot before chuckling softly.

"That daughter of mine," he said with obvious affection. "She's got you wrapped around her little finger... sure hope you're enjoying all the attention."

Cade felt heat rise in his cheeks but didn't deny the observation. Instead, he unfolded Eva's note and read it aloud: "'Come to me, all you who are weary and burdened, and I will give you rest.' Matthew 11:28."

"Hmm. Them's mighty strong words to live by," Chuck said as he continued working.

Chapter 33

Cade parked his truck in the gravel parking lot of Riverbend Valley Community Church, the engine ticking softly as it cooled in the evening air. He sat for a long moment, hands gripping the steering wheel as he stared at the white clapboard building that had once been a cornerstone in his life.

When was the last time he'd been inside? He couldn't even remember.

Cade climbed out of the truck and stood in the parking lot. He'd driven here on impulse after finishing the evening chores, drawn by Eva's latest scripture verse and the restless energy that had been building in him for days. But now that he was here, he wasn't sure what he'd hoped to accomplish.

The front doors were unlocked, opening with a gentle creak that echoed in the peaceful interior. The sanctuary was exactly as he remembered—wooden pews arranged in neat rows, stained glass windows depicting scenes from scripture, and a simple wooden cross hanging behind the altar.

"Cade?" Pastor Sam's voice carried from the altar. "What a pleasant surprise."

His wife, Virginia, looked up from where she'd been polishing the wooden communion table with him.

At forty-eight, Pastor Sam possessed the kind of gentle authority that put people at ease, while Virginia's smile radiated the warmth that had made her beloved by every congregation member.

"I'm sorry to interrupt," Cade said, suddenly self-conscious about his unannounced visit. "I can come back another time."

"Nonsense," Virginia said immediately, already gathering her cleaning supplies. "You're not interrupting anything that can't wait. I need to go clean Sam's office and fellowship hall anyway."

She squeezed Cade's arm as she passed. "It's good to see you here, dear."

Pastor Sam set down his polishing cloth and gestured toward the front pew. "Care to sit with me for a while? I could use an excuse to take a break from cleaning duties."

Cade nodded and settled onto the worn wooden pew that had hosted countless moments of prayer and contemplation over the decades.

"Pastor Sam," Cade said finally, his voice rough with emotion he couldn't quite hide. "Would you pray for me?"

"Of course. It would be my privilege."

Pastor Sam bowed his head. "Heavenly Father, we come before you tonight with grateful hearts, thanking you for bringing Cade here to this place of peace. We ask for your presence to fill this sanctuary and your love to surround him. Grant him clarity and strength. Help him to feel your nearness and to know that he is precious in your sight. In Jesus' name, amen."

"Amen," Cade whispered.

Pastor Sam settled back against the pew, his expression patient and open. "What's bothering you, son?"

The question opened a floodgate. "I'm lost. I've strayed so far from my faith that I don't even know how to find my way back. When I lost everything, I felt like God had abandoned me. Like maybe He never cared about me at all."

Pastor Sam nodded thoughtfully. "Feeling abandoned by God is one of the most painful experiences a person can have. But I've learned that sometimes when we can't feel His presence, it's not because He's moved away from us. Sometimes it's because pain has made us deaf to His voice."

"But how do you come back from pain? How do you trust again when everything you believed in gets destroyed?"

"One step at a time," Pastor Sam said gently. "Faith isn't a destination, Cade. It's a journey. And sometimes that journey takes us through valleys so dark we can't see the path ahead. But God is faithful even when we're not. He's been waiting patiently for you."

Cade stared at the cross behind the altar, wrestling with emotions that felt too big for words. "Eva's been giving me scripture verses every day for almost two weeks. At first, I thought it was just kindness. But now..." He paused, swallowing hard. "Now I think maybe God's been trying to get my attention."

"Sometimes God uses the people who love us to speak truth into our lives."

"I want to believe again," Cade admitted, his voice barely above a whisper. "I want to have the kind of faith that can weather storms and disappointments. But I don't know how to get there from where I am."

Pastor Sam was quiet for a moment, then turned to face Cade directly. "Faith isn't about never doubting, son. It's about choosing to trust even in the midst of doubt. It's about taking the next step forward even when you can't see where the path leads."

"Eva said something similar."

"Sounds like wisdom to me. Sometimes the bravest thing we can do is admit we're lost and ask for help finding our way home."

They sat in comfortable silence for several minutes, the peace of the sanctuary settling around them like a blessing. Through the stained glass windows, Cade could see the first stars beginning to appear in the darkening sky.

"Cade," Pastor Sam said finally, "pray with me."

Cade looked at the man who'd been shepherding this community for over a decade and nodded.

Pastor Sam bowed his head and spoke with quiet reverence. "Heavenly Father, we thank you for this moment of honesty and seeking. We ask that you meet Cade right where he is tonight—in his questions, in his hurt, in his desire to find his way back to you. Remind him that your love never fails, even when our faith wavers. Help him to trust one step at a time, to rest in your grace, and to know that you have good plans for his future. Give him peace in the uncertainty and strength for the journey ahead. We thank you for your patience and your faithfulness. In Jesus' name, amen."

"Amen," Cade whispered.

Pastor Sam reached over and patted Cade gently on the back, the simple gesture conveying more comfort than a dozen sermons. Cade stood and extended his hand, which Pastor Sam took in a firm, warm grip.

Without a word, Cade turned and walked quietly down the aisle toward the church doors, carrying with him a peace he hadn't felt in longer than he could remember.

Chapter 34

Friday, June 26th...

The supply room smelled of leather oil and grain dust. Cade stood before the metal shelving units that lined the walls, clipboard in hand, counting inventory and making notes about what needed to be ordered for the coming month.

"Let's see," he murmured, checking off items on his list. "Mineral supplements, check. Fly spray, running low. Salt blocks..." He paused to count the white blocks stacked on the bottom shelf, then made a note to order a dozen more.

The peaceful routine of the task suited his current frame of mind. Since his visit to the church last night, something had settled in his chest that felt like the peace Pastor Sam had prayed for. Not a complete transformation—he wasn't naive enough to think one conversation could undo months of spiritual struggle—but a quiet sense that maybe he was heading in the right direction.

The soft sound of footsteps approaching the tack room barely registered until a familiar voice spoke from the doorway.

"Working hard... or hardly working?"

Cade spun around, his heart doing that familiar skip it always performed when Eva appeared unexpectedly. Her smile was warm and slightly amused.

"You startled me," he said, setting his clipboard aside.

"Sorry." Eva said as she stepped into the room and reached into her jacket pocket. "Thought I'd deliver today's message in person again."

She extended a folded piece of paper toward him, and Cade walked toward her. When he was close enough to catch the scent of her perfume and see the flecks of gold in her blue eyes, he placed his hand over hers, covering her fingers with his palm.

"Eva," he said, his voice steadier than he'd expected. "Would you and Noah go to the rodeo with me tomorrow?"

Her eyes widened slightly, and for a moment they stood frozen in the quiet tack room, his hand warm over hers, the folded note forgotten between them. Then Eva's face broke into a smile so radiant it took his breath away.

"What took you so long to ask me?" she asked, her voice soft with laughter.

"Good point," he admitted, releasing her hand to take the note. "So tomorrow... I'll pick you both up around two?"

"Sounds like a plan," Eva said, already backing toward the doorway with barely contained excitement lighting her features. "See you then."

She turned and walked away with a spring in her step that made him smile. He'd done that—put that happiness in her voice and that bounce in her stride.

He looked down at the note in his hands and unfolded it:

"The Lord is my strength and my shield; my heart trusts in him, and he helps me." Psalm 28:7.

Chapter 35

Saturday, June 27th...

"Look at all the trailers with horses! And a bull? Did you see that bull, Cade? Mom, did you see the bull?" Noah's voice bounced around the cab of Cade's pickup like a pinball, his excitement so palpable it was practically vibrating through the seats.

Cade guided his truck into the dusty parking area of Riverbend Arena, the familiar grounds transformed into a bustling carnival of activity that drew visitors from several counties every summer. Horse trailers lined the back lot like a metallic city, while vendors' booths and colorful banners created a festive atmosphere that had Noah pressing his face against the window.

"Take a breath, sweetheart, before you hyperventilate," Eva laughed from the passenger seat, turning to smile at her son in the backseat.

"This is so cool! What's a rodeo like? Do cowboys ride bulls? Can we go see everything?"

Cade caught Eva's amused expression as he shut off the engine. "We'll see it all, little buddy. That's why we're here early—plenty of time to explore before the action starts."

The parking area buzzed with families unloading lawn chairs and coolers, teenagers in their best Western wear, and genuine cowboys preparing for competition. The air carried the scents of barbecue, hay, and that indefinable mixture of excitement that defined summer rodeos in Montana.

"Can we get out now? Please?" Noah was already working at his seatbelt buckles with the determination of a boy who'd spotted paradise just beyond the truck door.

"Slow down," Eva said gently. "No running off. You can get out of the truck, but you wait for us... got it?"

"Got it mom."

As Cade came around to help Eva down from the truck, she paused and reached into her purse, withdrawing a folded piece of paper.

"Before we go in," she said.

Cade unfolded the paper and read:

"Being confident of this, that he who began a good work in you will carry it on to completion until the day of Christ Jesus." Philippians 1:6.

He looked up to find her watching him with gentle expectation, and his smile came easily. "Thank you," he said, tucking the note safely in his shirt pocket as he turned to Noah. "Ready for your first rodeo?" he asked, extending his left hand to the boy who was bouncing with anticipation beside him.

Noah grabbed his hand immediately, his small fingers warm and trusting. Then, Cade held out his right hand to Eva.

She looked down at his outstretched palm for just a moment, then placed her hand in his with a smile. Her fingers were soft and warm, and when she gave his hand a gentle squeeze, Cade felt like he could conquer the world.

"Let's go see what all the fuss is about," he said as they walked toward the arena entrance.

The grounds were alive with the kind of organized chaotic fun that made small-town events special. A string quartet from the high school played patriotic songs from a makeshift bandstand, while the aroma of kettle corn and barbecue smoke created an irresistible combination that had Noah's head swiveling in all directions.

"Where should we start?" Eva asked.

"Anywhere Noah wants," Cade replied, noting how the boy's eyes had gone wide at the array of choices spread before them.

They wandered through the vendor booths first, Noah marveling at everything from hand-tooled leather belts to wooden toys carved in the shapes of horses and cattle. At a booth selling Western wear, Cade stopped and studied a display of children's cowboy hats.

"What do you think, partner?" he asked Noah, lifting a small black hat from the display. "Every cowboy needs proper headgear."

Noah's eyes went wide as Cade settled the hat on his head, adjusting the brim with careful attention. "Really? For me?"

"Course," Cade said, handing money to the smiling vendor before Eva could even think to object. "Can't take you to your first rodeo without the right equipment."

Eva's expression was soft with gratitude as she watched Noah preen in his new hat, standing taller and somehow looking older.

"What do you say, Noah?" Eva prompted gently.

"Thank you, Cade! This is the best hat ever!" Noah threw his arms around Cade's waist in an impulsive hug that made something warm and wonderful unfold in his chest.

They continued their exploration, stopping at a booth selling handmade soaps where Eva lingered over lavender and vanilla scents while Noah investigated a display of wooden puzzles.

"These are beautiful," Eva said, holding up a bar of soap that smelled like wildflowers.

"Pick out a few," Cade said.

"Cade—"

"I want you to," he said simply, his hand finding the small of her back in a gesture that felt both protective and intimate.

The gentle pressure of his palm against her back sent warmth spiraling through Eva's chest, and she found herself nodding without argument.

The petting zoo proved to be Noah's favorite discovery, a fenced area where children could interact with gentle farm animals under the watchful eyes of teenage volunteers. Noah immediately gravitated toward a friendly goat who seemed equally interested in him, while Eva and Cade leaned against the fence rails to watch.

"He rarely got to see farm animals up close like this when we lived in the city," Eva said, her voice soft with maternal affection as Noah giggled at the goat's attempts to eat his new hat.

"He's a natural," Cade observed, watching Noah confidently pet a lamb while asking the volunteer detailed questions about sheep farming. "Most kids his age are either scared or too aggressive. He's got the right instincts."

Eva glanced sideways at Cade, noting the pride in his voice when he talked about Noah. "He adores you, you know. You've become his hero."

The words created a tightness in Cade's throat that had nothing to do with the dust in the air.

"You're good with him," Eva continued, her hand finding his arm in a touch that was brief but deliberate. "Better than you probably realize."

Before Cade could respond, Noah came racing over with dirt on his knees and joy radiating from his small frame. "Did you see me with the baby calf? He tried to suck on my fingers! And the lady said I could help feed the chickens if I wanted to!"

"Sounds like fun," Cade said, ruffling the boy's hair beneath his new hat. "Better get over there before they run out of chicken feed."

Afterward, they spent the next couple of hours exploring every corner of the festival grounds. They sampled funnel cake that left powdered sugar on Noah's cheeks, watched a blacksmith demonstration that had all three of them fascinated by the ancient craft, and browsed through more booths selling everything from homemade jam to intricately beaded jewelry.

At a game booth where players tried to toss rings over bottles, Cade stepped up and handed money to the operator. "Pick your prize, Noah," he said, nodding toward the stuffed animals hanging from the booth's ceiling.

"The horse!" Noah pointed to a plush palomino that looked remarkably like one of the ranch horses. "Can you really win it?"

"We'll find out," Cade said, accepting the rings from the game operator.

Eva watched with growing admiration as Cade took his time, studying the bottles and calculating angles with the same careful attention he brought to ranch work. His first throw missed by inches, but the second ring settled neatly over a bottle neck with a satisfying clink.

"One more," the operator said encouragingly.

Cade's third throw was perfect, the ring dropping cleanly over another bottle. The operator grinned and reached for the stuffed horse, presenting it to Noah with a flourish.

"You did it!" Noah clutched the horse to his chest like a treasure.

"What are you going to name him?" Eva asked, her heart full as she watched her son's happiness.

"Storm," Noah said immediately. "Is that okay?"

"That's perfect," Cade answered.

As they wandered toward the arena entrance, Noah chattering about everything he'd seen and experienced, Eva found herself stealing glances at the man walking beside her. This was the Cade she'd fallen in love with at seventeen, but better—more mature, more deliberate in his kindness, and more aware of the precious nature of moments like these.

When his hand found hers again as they navigated through the crowd, Eva didn't hesitate to intertwine their fingers. The simple gesture felt natural and right, like pieces of a puzzle finally clicking into place.

The afternoon sun was beginning to slant lower in the sky, painting everything in golden light that made the festival atmosphere even more magical. Families were beginning to migrate toward the arena seating, while cowboys made final preparations for the evening's competition.

"Look at all the people," Noah marveled, his eyes wide as they approached the arena entrance where lines were beginning to form.

"Saturday night rodeos are always a big draw," Cade explained, pulling their printed tickets from his shirt pocket. "Folks come from all over the county."

"You bought tickets already?" Eva asked, noting official markings.

"Online," Cade confirmed with a small smile that spoke of careful planning.

The announcement came crackling over the PA system just as they reached the entrance gates: "Ladies and gentlemen, welcome to the annual Riverbend Rodeo! Please make your way to your seats. Tonight's competition begins in ten minutes!"

Noah bounced on his toes, clutching his stuffed horse and looking up at Cade with worship in his eyes. "This is the best day ever!"

Cade looked down at the boy, then over at Eva, whose smile was soft with gratitude and something deeper that made his pulse quicken. "Yeah," he said quietly, meaning it more than he'd meant anything in a long time. "It really is."

Chapter 36

"Where do we sit?" Noah's voice carried pure amazement as Cade led them up the wooden bleachers toward their reserved spots, prime seating just four rows back from the arena fence that would give them an unobstructed view of all the action.

"Right here," Cade confirmed, checking the ticket numbers against the bench seats. "Best view in the house."

The arena buzzed with anticipation as families filled the stands around them. Noah clutched his stuffed horse and swiveled his head in every direction, trying to take in everything at once—the cowboys preparing their equipment near the chutes, the horses being led around the perimeter, and the officials checking safety gear with practiced efficiency.

"How do they stay on?" Noah asked, pointing toward a cowboy stretching beside a chute where a bronc snorted and pawed the ground. "The horses look really mad."

"That's the whole point," Cade explained, settling back against the bleacher bench with his arm stretched along the back, his fingers just brushing Eva's shoulder. "The horses are bred and trained to buck. The cowboys try to stay on for eight seconds using only one hand."

"Eight seconds?" Noah's eyes went wide.

"You'd be surprised how long eight seconds can feel when you're on the back of a bucking horse," Eva said with a laugh.

The PA system crackled to life, and the announcer's voice boomed across the arena. "Ladies and gentlemen, welcome to the thirty-seventh annual Riverbend Rodeo! Please rise for our national anthem."

The crowd stood as one, hats coming off heads in a wave of respect that rippled through the stands. Noah immediately removed his new cowboy hat, mimicking the adults around him, while a local high school student stepped into the arena with a microphone. Her clear, strong voice carried "The Star-Spangled Banner" across the evening air, and Eva felt a familiar tightness in her throat at the sight of three hundred people united in quiet reverence.

When the anthem ended, Pastor Sam appeared in the arena center for the traditional opening prayer. "Heavenly Father, we thank you for this beautiful evening and the opportunity to gather as a community. Watch over our cowboys and cowgirls tonight, keep them safe, and let this be an evening of good sportsmanship and fellowship. In your name we pray, amen."

"Amen," echoed through the stands, and Eva caught Cade quietly joining in. The small gesture made her heart flutter with hope for the healing she'd been praying for.

"And now, ladies and gentlemen, please welcome our Grand Entry!" the announcer called.

The arena gates swung open, and Noah gasped as riders thundered in carrying American flags, state flags, and colorful banners that snapped in the wind created by their horses' movement. The parade circled the arena to upbeat country music, riders whooping and waving to the crowd while their mounts pranced and danced with barely contained energy.

"I want to do that one day," Noah said, his voice filled with wonder as a young rider on a paint horse galloped past their section.

"Maybe you will," Cade said.

"Can we get some food?" Noah asked as vendors began moving through the stands with their offerings. "I'm hungry, and everything smells so good."

"What looks good?" Cade asked, reaching for his wallet as a vendor approached with a tray full of nachos and chili dogs he balanced with ease.

"Everything!" Noah exclaimed, making both adults laugh.

They settled on chili dogs, nachos to share, and cold lemonade that came in plastic cups featuring the rodeo logo.

"First event up is bareback bronc riding!" the announcer called. "Our first rider is Jed Feltcher from Billings, Montana, on a horse named Tornado!"

The chute gate exploded open, and Noah nearly jumped out of his seat as a bay horse launched himself into the arena, bucking and spinning with wild determination while the cowboy held on with just one hand, his other arm waving for balance. Eight seconds seemed to last forever as horse and rider engaged in their ancient dance of strength and will.

"He stayed on!" Noah shouted when the buzzer sounded, and pickup riders moved in to help the cowboy dismount safely. "Did you see that?"

"Solid ride," Cade said, wiping a smear of ketchup from Noah's chin with his napkin.

They watched rider after rider attempt their eight-second battles, some successful, others hitting the dirt in spectacular fashion that had

Noah alternately gasping and cheering. Cade explained the scoring system, the techniques for staying balanced, and the different styles of horses with the patient expertise of someone who understood the sport from the inside out.

"Remember when we were in high school, and you were convinced you could master it?" Eva said during a lull between riders, smiling at the memory.

Cade groaned and shook his head. "That lasted exactly one practice session. Turns out there's a big difference between riding broke horses and broncs that don't want you on their backs."

"How long did you stay on?" Noah asked with fascination.

"About two seconds," Cade admitted, earning delighted laughter from Noah. "I ended up with a face full of arena dirt and a bruised back. Decided I was better suited to working cattle."

"Smart man," Eva said.

The saddle bronc riding followed, with riders using saddles and longer stirrups that allowed for different techniques and more dramatic rides. Noah was completely absorbed, asking questions about everything from the horses' breeding to the cowboys' protective gear.

"Why do some horses buck higher than others?" he wanted to know.

"Breeding and training," Cade explained. "Some bloodlines are known for producing strong buckers. And the horses learn the job just like the cowboys do—experience makes them better at it."

When the barrel racing began, Noah's attention shifted to the female competitors who raced their horses in tight patterns around three barrels set in a triangle. The speed was breathtaking, horses and riders working in perfect harmony as they shaved fractions of seconds off their times.

"They're going so fast!" Noah marveled as a local rider named Sarah Beth Williams took the lead with a blazing 16.8-second run. "How do they not fall off?"

"Balance and trust," Eva said, remembering her own barrel racing days in high school. "Horse and rider have to work as a team."

"Did you ever do that, Mom?"

"A few times," Eva admitted. "Not very well, but it was fun. I gave it a shot, and I'll never regret trying."

"She's being modest," Cade said, his hand finding hers where it rested on her knee. "She won a second-place ribbon at the county fair our junior year."

"You won a ribbon, Mom?" Noah's excitement was infectious. "Do you still have it?"

"In my old room at Grandma and Grandpa's house. It's still hanging on my pegboard."

The afternoon progressed through team roping, steer wrestling, and calf roping, each event bringing new explanations from Cade and endless questions from Noah. During the steer wrestling, Noah misheard the announcer's explanation about "bulldogging" and asked innocently, "Why would anyone want to fight a bulldog?"

The confusion sent all three of them into fits of laughter that had other spectators turning to smile at their obvious enjoyment. Cade's deep chuckle mixed with Eva's lighter laughter and Noah's giggles, creating the kind of moment that felt perfect and unrepeatable.

"It's not an actual dog," Eva explained when they finally caught their breath. "It's just the name for tackling a steer from horseback."

"Ohhhh," Noah said seriously.

As the sun began to set behind the mountains, painting the sky in brilliant shades of orange and pink, the final event approached. The bull riding drew the biggest crowds and the loudest cheers, and Noah was practically vibrating with excitement as the first rider prepared to mount his bull.

"This is the most dangerous event," Cade explained, his free hand resting protectively on Noah's shoulder. "Bulls are bigger and stronger than horses, and they're usually more unpredictable."

"Are the cowboys scared?" Noah asked, watching a rider wrap his hand in the bull rope with ritualistic precision.

"If they're smart, they're at least a little nervous," Cade said. "Fear keeps you alert. But they train for this, and they know how to fall safely."

The chute gate opened, and a massive black bull exploded into the arena, spinning and kicking with such violence that Noah unconsciously leaned closer to Cade for security. The cowboy lasted six seconds before being thrown clear, rolling away from the bull's hooves while rodeo clowns moved in to distract the animal.

"Wow," Noah breathed, clutching his stuffed horse tighter. "That's scary."

"That's bull riding," Eva said, remembering the mixture of terror and fascination she'd felt watching these same events as a child.

They watched the remaining riders, some lasting the full eight seconds, others hitting the dirt in spectacular fashion that had the crowd cheering and groaning in equal measure. Through it all, Cade's hand remained warm and steady in Eva's, their joined fingers resting against her knee in a gesture that felt both intimate and comfortably natural.

When the final bull rider completed his attempt and the arena lights began to dim, signaling the end of the competition, Noah sat back against the bleacher with a satisfied sigh.

"Best day ever," he declared, throwing his arms around Cade's waist in a fierce hug.

Cade returned the hug with obvious emotion, his voice slightly rough when he spoke. "Yeah, it has been."

Then, in a gesture that made Eva's heart stop completely, Cade raised their still-joined hands to his lips and pressed a gentle kiss to her knuckles. The contact was soft and reverent, lasting just long enough to make her breath catch and her pulse race, before he lowered their hands back to rest against her knee.

In that moment, surrounded by the lingering sounds of celebration and the scent of arena dust, Eva knew with absolute certainty that whatever was growing between them was worth every ounce of her patience as Cade found his way again.

Chapter 37

*S*unday, June 28th...

"Remember to put your offering in the plate when it comes around," Eva whispered to Noah as they settled into their usual pew beside her parents. The familiar sanctuary buzzed with quiet conversation and the rustle of programs while families found their seats for Sunday morning worship.

"I've got my dollar here," Noah whispered back, patting his shirt pocket.

Eva smiled and smoothed his hair, noting how handsome he looked in his Sunday clothes—khaki pants, a blue button-down shirt, and the little tie that her dad had taught him to knot himself. The past few weeks had been full of so many changes and new experiences that she wondered if Noah even realized how much his world had expanded since they'd moved here.

"Cade!"

Noah's excited exclamation drew Eva's attention to the center aisle, where she looked to see Cade making his way toward their pew. Her eyes widened at the sight of him—clean-shaven, wearing a white button-down shirt that fit his broad shoulders perfectly, a bolo tie, and dark jeans.

The expression on his face made her pulse quicken.

"Morning," Cade said softly, his smile warm as he nodded to Chuck and Ruby before settling beside Eva. She caught the scent of his cologne mixed with the smell of soap and sunshine that always seemed to cling to him.

"Well, look who decided to join us," Chuck said with obvious pleasure, leaning forward. "Good to see you here, son."

"About time," Ruby added. "We've been saving you a seat for months... I knew one day you'd come back."

Noah scrambled over to claim Cade's lap, settling against him with the easy trust that had developed between them. Cade's arms went around the boy automatically, and Eva felt her heart squeeze at the picture they made together.

"Pastor Sam told us about David fighting the giant last week," Noah whispered.

"I remember that story," Cade said quietly.

The organ music began to play, signaling the start of service, and Eva opened the Bible on her lap. She withdrew the folded piece of paper she'd placed there this morning after finishing it.

Cade accepted the note with a grin that made her stomach flutter, unfolding it carefully while Pastor Sam made his way to the pulpit. Eva watched his face as he read the verse she'd chosen:

"Therefore, my dear brothers and sisters, stand firm. Let nothing move you. Always give yourselves fully to the work of the Lord, because you know that your labor in the Lord is not in vain." 1 Corinthians 15:58

"Good morning, friends," Pastor Sam's voice carried across the sanctuary, warm and welcoming as always. His gaze swept across the congregation, pausing when he spotted Cade among the Turner family. His smile widened noticeably.

"You know," Pastor Sam continued, setting aside his prepared notes, "I had planned to speak about something entirely different this morning. But looking out at all of you, I feel moved to talk about something else instead. About God's unfailing love and how He never gives up on us."

A chorus of amens rose from the congregation, and Eva felt Cade's slight movement beside her as he adjusted Noah on his lap.

Pastor Sam spoke with his usual gentle authority about prodigal sons and patient fathers, about wandering sheep and faithful shepherds who never stopped searching. His words seemed to flow directly to the hearts that needed them most, and Eva found herself praying silently for the man beside her who was hearing these truths with ears that had been deaf for too long.

Halfway through the sermon, when Pastor Sam was talking about the joy in heaven over one sinner who repents, she reached over and covered his free hand with hers.

Cade's fingers turned palm up, accepting her touch and intertwining their fingers. Noah leaned more fully against Cade's chest, and for a moment Eva had a glimpse of what their future might look like—Sunday mornings spent together as a family, sharing faith and fellowship and the quiet joy of belonging to something larger than themselves.

The sermon continued with stories of redemption and restoration, of second chances and divine patience that never runs out.

When the final hymn ended and Pastor Sam offered the closing blessing, Eva felt a sense of completion that had nothing to do with the church service and everything to do with the man beside her who'd found the courage to step back into faith.

The congregation began to file out slowly, and the usual Sunday morning ritual of handshakes and brief conversations occurred. Pastor Sam and Virginia stood at the back doors, offering personal goodbyes to each family as they left.

"That was a good sermon," Cade said as they gathered their things and prepared to join the line moving toward the exit.

"Pastor Sam has a gift for knowing exactly what people need to hear," Eva replied.

When they reached the back of the church, Pastor Sam's face lit up at the sight of Cade approaching. The handshake he offered was firm and warm, but it was his words that made Eva's throat tighten with emotion.

"Welcome home, son," Pastor Sam said, his voice thick with genuine feeling. "Welcome home."

Before Cade could respond, Pastor Sam pulled him into a tight bear hug that lasted several heartbeats and conveyed more love and acceptance than a dozen sermons could have managed. When they separated, Eva saw moisture in Cade's eyes.

"Thank you," Cade said simply, his voice rough with emotion he wasn't trying to hide.

"Thank you for coming," Pastor Sam replied. "Your presence here matters more than you know."

As they walked toward the parking lot together, Eva felt a sense of rightness settle over her like a blessing. This was what she'd been praying for, what she'd hoped her daily messages might help accomplish. Not just Cade's return to church, but his return to the faith that had once anchored his life and could do so again.

The morning sun was warm on their faces, and Noah's chatter about lunch plans filled the air. But Eva's attention was focused on the man walking beside her, noting the peace in his expression and the lightness in his step that spoke of burdens being set down.

"So... wanna come over for lunch?" she asked.

"I had something else in mind," he said. "Go on home and change and meet me at your mom and dad's horse barn in about an hour."

Chapter 38

Three horses stood saddled and ready outside the barn, their bridles gleaming in the afternoon sunlight. Cade checked Storm's girth one final time, then picked up the wicker picnic basket that hung on a fence post, thinking of Lily Hawthorne's knowing smile when he'd stopped by the Bluebird Café after church to pick up his order. He was grateful for her willingness to have everything ready on such short notice.

The sound of approaching voices had him turning to see Eva and Noah approaching.

"You've been busy," Eva said, her smile warm as she took in the scene. "When did you have time to saddle three horses?"

"I hustled," Cade admitted.

Eva peered into the basket after he handed it to her, her eyebrows rising. "Where did all this come from?"

"I might have placed an order at the Bluebird Café," Cade said with a grin.

"You planned this whole day, didn't you?".

"Seemed like a good day for a ride," Cade replied.

"Can we go now?" Noah asked.

Cade helped Noah mount first, checking his stirrups and making sure he was secure in the saddle. "You remember everything we practiced?"

"Keep my heels down and hands steady," Noah recited with the seriousness of someone proving he'd been paying attention.

"Good man," Cade said, then moved to help Eva mount Buttercup.

His hands were steady and sure as he held the stirrup for her, though he was acutely aware of the brief contact when she placed her hand on his shoulder for balance. She settled into the saddle with ease.

"Where are we going?" Eva asked as Cade swung up onto Storm and secured the picnic basket.

"You'll see," Cade replied, guiding Storm toward the trail that led away from the ranch buildings.

The ride to the creek took them through some of the most beautiful country in the valley, rolling pastures dotted with wildflowers and framed by the distant peaks of the mountains surrounding them. Noah chattered excitedly about everything he saw, pointing out hawks circling overhead and asking detailed questions about the cattle they passed.

When they reached the familiar spot where Lost Creek meandered through a grove of cottonwood trees, Cade felt a sense of rightness settle over him.

"I love it here," Eva said as they dismounted near the large, smooth boulder that overlooked the water.

Cade spread the blanket he'd grabbed from his house while Eva helped Noah tie Daisy to a sturdy branch. The horses immediately began grazing on the tender grass that grew thick along the creek bank, their contentment adding to the peaceful atmosphere.

"Let's see what we have for lunch," Eva said, opening the basket and removing three individual styrofoam to-go containers holding crispy fried chicken, creamy pasta salad, and thick brownies. Bottles of water, napkins, and plastic silverware were tucked in the bottom of the basket.

"This is good," Noah declared around a bite of chicken.

"Sure is," Cade agreed.

They ate, with Noah providing running commentary about everything from the taste of the pasta salad to his observations about the minnows visible in the shallow water of the creek. The afternoon sun was warm without being oppressive, and a gentle breeze rustled the cottonwood leaves above them.

After the food was consumed and remaining empty containers carefully packed away, Cade and Eva leaned back on their elbows, watching Noah explore the creek bank with the fearless curiosity of childhood. He had rolled up his jeans on his own and waded into the shallow water, hunting for interesting rocks and probably scaring away every fish for miles with his enthusiastic splashing.

"This has been the most wonderful day," Eva said, her voice carrying the kind of contentment that came from perfect moments. "Thanks for planning it."

"You deserve it," Cade admitted, pleased by the peace in her expression.

They sat in comfortable silence for a few minutes, both enjoying the sight of Noah's innocent joy and the peaceful sounds of running water and birdsong. It was Eva who broke the silence with a suggestion that made Cade's pulse quicken.

"You know," she said, turning slightly to face him, "I've been thinking it might be nice if you came by for coffee in the mornings before you start work. I get up early anyway, and I'd enjoy the company."

The invitation was casual, but Cade heard the deeper meaning behind it—a desire for more time together.

"I'd like that. What time works for you?"

"Seven?"

"Seven it is," Cade agreed, already looking forward to starting his mornings with Eva's smile and genuine conversation.

"Come play!" Noah called from the creek.

Eva laughed and stood, extending her hand to Cade. "What do you say? Think we can handle getting our feet wet?"

Cade took her hand and let her pull him to his feet. "I think we can manage that."

They kicked off their boots and socks and rolled up their jeans before wading into the creek to join Noah. The water was surprisingly warm, heated by the afternoon sun as it flowed over the smooth stones that lined the creek bed.

What started as cautious wading quickly escalated into playful splashing when Noah discovered that cupping his hands created the perfect water launcher. Soon all three of them were engaged in an impromptu water fight, laughter echoing across the peaceful valley as they dodged and retaliated with increasing enthusiasm.

"You're getting soaked!" Eva called to Cade, her own shirt spotted with water and her hair escaping its ponytail in damp tendrils.

"So are you!" Cade replied, sending a gentle splash in her direction that made her shriek with laughter.

In her attempt to dodge his latest assault, Eva stepped backward onto a moss-covered rock and felt her foot slip. She would have fallen hard if Cade hadn't moved with lightning reflexes, catching her around the waist and pulling her against his chest before she could hit the water.

For a moment they stood frozen, her hands braced against his shoulders, his arms secure around her waist, their faces inches apart. Eva's laughter faded as she looked up into his eyes, her breath catching and her pulse racing.

"I've got you," Cade said.

"I know," Eva said, her gaze dropping to his lips for just a moment before meeting his eyes again.

The kiss was inevitable, as natural as breathing. Cade lowered his head slowly, giving her every opportunity to pull away, but Eva remained perfectly still as his lips touched hers. The contact was soft and sweet, lasting just long enough to promise everything.

When they separated, Eva's eyes were bright with wonder and something that looked very much like joy.

"Is that what cowboys do when moms almost fall down?"

Cade and Eva sprang apart, both of them flushing with embarrassment and poorly suppressed laughter. Eva recovered first, moving toward Noah with the kind of diplomatic grace that only mothers possessed.

"Sometimes," she said with admirable composure, "when a cowboy cares about someone very much, he might give a girl a special kiss to make sure she's okay."

"Like when you kiss my scraped knees?" Noah asked with the logic of an eight-year-old trying to understand adult behavior.

"Something like that," Eva agreed, shooting Cade a look that was pure amusement.

"Cool," Noah said with satisfaction, already losing interest in adult romance in favor of the much more exciting prospect of finding crawdads under the rocks.

Cade met Eva's eyes, both of them fighting smiles at Noah's easy acceptance of the situation. The afternoon sun continued to shine, the water continued to babble peacefully around their feet, and somewhere in the distance a bird called with liquid notes that sounded remarkably like a benediction.

Some moments, Cade realized, were perfect just as they were—complete with interrupted kisses, curious little boys, and the promise of many more afternoons exactly like this one.

Chapter 39

*M*onday, June 29th...

"Morning," Cade said as he climbed the porch steps of the bed and breakfast, noting how Eva's smile made the early hour feel like a gift rather than an obligation.

She sat curled in one of the wicker chairs, coffee cup in hand. Her Bible lay open on the small table beside her with a folded slip of paper on top, and a second coffee cup waited beside it.

"Right on time," Eva said, reaching for the extra cup and extending it toward him. "Black, just like you used to take it."

He accepted the coffee gratefully, savoring both the rich aroma and the thoughtfulness behind the gesture.

"Thanks," he said, settling into the chair across from her.

Eva looked out over the valley that stretched toward the distant mountains, her expression peaceful as she took in the view that never seemed to lose its power to inspire. "Look at that," she said quietly.

Cade followed her gaze, taking in the rolling pastures where morning mist clung to the low places and the first cattle of the day moved like dark shapes against the golden grass. The mountains rose beyond it all, their peaks catching the early sunlight and painting the sky in shades of rose and gold.

"What a view," he said, though he found himself watching her profile more than the landscape. There was something about Eva in the morning light, coffee cup cradled in her hands and contentment written across her features, that made him grateful.

"What are you doing on the ranch today?" Eva asked, turning her attention back to him with genuine interest.

"Moving cattle," Cade replied, taking a sip of coffee. "Your dad wants to move a few herds before the grass gets overgrazed. Should take most of the morning if we don't have any strays that decide to be difficult."

"And this afternoon?"

"Fence repair in the north section." He paused, then asked, "What about you? Any exciting plans for today?"

Eva's face lit up with the kind of enthusiasm that came from talking about work she genuinely loved. "Marketing and advertisements, mostly. I need to update the website with new photos and descriptions, post on social media, and maybe reach out to some travel bloggers who feature Montana destinations. Lots of computer work."

"Sounds like you've got it all figured out," Cade said.

"I hope so," Eva replied with a laugh. "Opening a bed and breakfast is more complicated than I realized, but I'm learning."

She reached for the folded piece of paper on top of her Bible, extending it across the table with a gentle smile. Cade opened the note and read aloud:

"*'Your word is a lamp for my feet, a light on my path.' Psalm 119:105.*"

He smiled at her as he folded the paper and tucked it into his shirt pocket.

Eva finished the last of her coffee and stood, stretching with the fluid grace of someone ready to tackle whatever the day might bring. "Now go get to work, cowboy," she said with a playful grin that made his pulse quicken.

She gathered her Bible and coffee cup and headed toward the front door, leaving him sitting alone on the porch with his coffee and the echo of her voice. Cade shook his head with amusement, already looking forward to tomorrow morning's coffee date with her.

Chapter 40

Tuesday, June 30th...

"Morning," Cade said as he reached the top of the porch steps. She sat with her Bible balanced on her lap. A second cup of coffee waited on the table beside her, accompanied by a Ziploc bag of what appeared to be trail mix.

"Coffee tastes perfect this morning," Eva replied, gesturing toward the chair across from her.

Cade settled into his seat and reached for the coffee, savoring the rich aroma.

"I tested out a new trail mix recipe yesterday evening," Eva said, pointing to the Ziploc bag. "That's for you today while you're out working. Almonds, dried cranberries, oatmeal clusters, and a few other things. Figured you might get hungry between meals."

"Thanks," he said, picking up the bag and noting the generous portion she'd prepared. "Looks good."

"So what's on your agenda today."

"Paperwork this morning," Cade said, taking a sip of perfectly prepared coffee. "Need to catch up on some records and supply orders. I have to run into town for a few parts for the tractor. Then your dad and I are going to finalize plans for buying another forty head of cattle."

"Hmmm... big day... more cattle means more work."

"Some, but the ranch hands can handle it. Market prices are good right now," Cade paused, then asked, "What about you? More marketing work today?"

Eva's expression shifted to something that looked like barely contained excitement. "Actually, I had an interesting conversation yesterday. A virtual meeting with another bed and breakfast owner I connected with on social media. She runs a place a few hours north of here."

"How'd that go?"

"Really well. She shared numerous tips and tricks about everything from booking systems to guest amenities. But the most interesting part was learning about how she's expanded her business." Eva leaned forward slightly, her enthusiasm evident. "She just added tiny homes to her property and started offering dude ranch experiences. Guests can stay in the tiny homes and learn about ranch life—horseback riding, cattle work, and other activities."

Cade set down his coffee cup, intrigued. "Dude ranch experiences?"

"Yep, her packages offer basic horsemanship, trail rides, and learning to rope, and guests can even participate in a cattle drive if they want and learn to muck stalls. She partners with a local ranch for the activities, but the guests stay on her property in these beautiful little tiny homes that feel like luxury camping."

"And people actually pay for that?"

Eva laughed at his expression. "Apparently. She said city folks are hungry for authentic experiences, for the chance to disconnect from technology and learn traditional skills. She's booked solid through next summer."

Cade found himself considering the concept more seriously. The idea of sharing ranch knowledge with people who genuinely wanted to learn was appealing, and he could see how Eva's natural hospitality would make such an operation successful.

"You thinking about trying something like that here?" he asked.

"Maybe. I want to do some more research on it. Talk to Mom and Dad and get their thoughts. I'd need to partner with someone who actually knows ranch work." Eva's gaze met his meaningfully. "Someone who could teach guests the real skills, not just the tourist version."

"Sounds interesting," he said.

"It's exciting to think about... which is exactly what I want you to do. Think on it while you're out working. What would something like that involve? How much manpower would it take? It's just an idea... I'd need to get this place opened up first... then maybe... oh well, you just never know where an idea like this could go."

They sat in comfortable silence for a moment, both contemplating possibilities that felt within reach. The morning sun climbed higher, reminding them both that the day's responsibilities were waiting.

"Well," Eva said as she stretched, "let's get our day started."

She reached into her jeans pocket and withdrew a folded piece of paper, extending it toward him.

Cade unfolded the note and read aloud:

"'Let us not become weary in doing good, for at the proper time we will reap a harvest if we do not give up.' Galatians 6:9."

The verse felt particularly relevant after their conversation about future plans and possibilities. Cade stood, folded the paper, and slipped it into his shirt pocket. He set his coffee cup down, grabbed the bag of trail mix, and stepped toward Eva.

When he reached her chair, he extended his hand, palm up. Eva looked at him with surprise but placed her hand in his without hesitation. Cade lifted her fingers to his lips and pressed a gentle kiss on her knuckles.

Eva's cheeks flushed pink, but her smile was radiant. "Aren't you the romantic."

Cade released her hand and turned toward the porch steps, feeling her gaze follow him as he walked away.

"Have a good day," Eva called after him.

Chapter 41

Wednesday, July 1st...

"Mornin', beautiful," Cade said as he climbed the porch steps.

She sat curled in her usual wicker chair, wearing a soft pink blouse and jeans, her Bible balanced on her lap and her hair catching the golden sunrise. A to-go cup of coffee waited on the table beside her.

"Morning yourself, handsome," Eva replied with a smile that made his heart skip.

Cade settled into his chair and reached for the coffee cup, marveling at how this simple morning ritual had become the best part of his day.

"Sleep well?" he asked, noting the peaceful contentment in her expression as she gazed out over the valley where morning mist still clung to the low places.

"Really well," Eva admitted. "What's on your agenda today?"

"Moving the bred heifers to the closer pasture," Cade replied, taking a sip of coffee that was, as always, exactly how he liked it. "Your dad wants them where we can keep a closer eye on them as they get closer to calving season. Should be an easy morning if they cooperate."

"And this afternoon?"

"Paperwork. A run into town to pick up supplies. Then... actually, I was hoping to spend some time researching that dude ranch idea you mentioned yesterday," Cade said, watching her face light up with excitement.

Eva's smile was radiant. "Sounds like an interesting afternoon for you then."

"What about you?" he asked.

"More website work," Eva said, though her enthusiasm was obvious. "I want to add a section about local attractions and activities. Then research the dude ranch concept some more. Mom's coming over this afternoon, and I'm going to run the idea by her as well."

Eva finished the last of her coffee and stood, stretching with the fluid grace that never failed to make his pulse quicken. She reached into her jeans pocket and withdrew a folded piece of paper, but instead of handing it across the table as she usually did, she walked over to his chair.

Cade looked up at her, noting the way the morning light created a halo effect around her hair and the gentle smile meant just for him. When she extended the note, he took it with one hand while catching her fingers with the other.

"Eva," he said softly, not releasing her hand. "Thank you. For everything you've done for me these past weeks. The notes, the patience, the way you've helped me find my way back to..." He paused, struggling with words that felt too small for what he wanted to express.

"Back to yourself," Eva finished gently, her free hand coming up to touch his cheek with butterfly softness.

The tenderness in her touch, the absolute certainty in her voice, made something inside him break open.

"I don't know what I did to deserve you," he said, his voice rough with emotion.

"You don't have to deserve love, Cade," Eva said simply. "You just have to be willing to accept it."

She leaned down and pressed a soft kiss to his forehead, the gesture so tender and full of promise that Cade felt his eyes burn with tears. When she straightened, her smile was soft with love and hope.

"Now go get to work, cowboy," she said with playful affection. "Those heifers won't move themselves."

Eva headed toward the front door, pausing to look back at him with an expression that made his heart race. "See you tomorrow morning?"

"Wouldn't miss it," Cade said, meaning it more than he'd ever meant anything in his life.

He watched her disappear inside the house, then unfolded the note she'd given him.

"He will cover you with his feathers, and under his wings you will find refuge; his faithfulness will be your shield and rampart." Psalm 91:4

Chapter 42

"Morning, sunshine," Cade said as he approached the porch, breathing in the heavenly aroma of fresh-baked goods that drifted from the house.

Eva looked up from her Bible with a smile that made his heart do that familiar skip. She wore a soft blue sundress that brought out her eyes, and her hair was pulled back with a few loose tendrils framing her face. The sight of her sitting there in the golden morning light, surrounded by the scent of apple and cinnamon, felt like stepping into a dream he'd never dared to have.

"Hey... good mornin'," Eva said, immediately reaching for the folded paper beside her coffee cup.

She stood and met him at the top of the porch steps, extending the note with a smile that held both mischief and tenderness. "Read this one right away. I think you'll understand why."

Cade accepted the paper, noting how her fingers lingered against his for just a moment longer than necessary. He unfolded it and read aloud:

"Because of the Lord's great love we are not consumed, for his compassions never fail. They are new every morning; great is your faithfulness."
Lamentations 3:22–23

He looked up to find Eva watching him.

"New every morning," she said softly. "I've been thinking about that phrase. How every sunrise is God giving us a fresh start, a clean slate. No matter what happened yesterday, we get to begin again."

Cade folded the note, his throat tight with emotion. "I needed to hear that today," he admitted. "I had a rough day yesterday. Sometimes I forget that I don't have to drag all of that into today."

Eva reached for his hand and gave it a gentle squeeze. This woman had a gift for knowing exactly what his soul needed to hear.

"Now," Eva said with renewed brightness, "I hope you're hungry because I felt like baking this morning."

She led him to the table where a basket covered with a cheerful yellow cloth sat beside their coffee cups. When she lifted the cloth, the scent of apple spice muffins made his stomach growl audibly.

"Apple spice?" Cade asked, settling into his chair and accepting the coffee cup she handed him.

"Yep," Eva confirmed, selecting a muffin and breaking it open to reveal the tender, fragrant interior. "My grandma's recipe. She used to make them every fall when the apples were ready."

Cade bit into his muffin and closed his eyes as the flavors exploded in his mouth. Warm spices, sweet, tender apple pieces, and the perfect crunchy crumb topping.

"This is incredible," he said, opening his eyes to find Eva watching him.

"Food tastes better when it's made with love," she said simply.

They ate in comfortable silence for a few minutes, both savoring the muffins and the peaceful morning atmosphere. A meadowlark called somewhere in the distance, and the gentle breeze carried the scent of wildflowers from the meadow beyond the house.

"What's gonna keep you busy today?" Eva asked.

"Hay delivery this morning," Cade replied. "We're getting the first cutting from the Johnson place. Should keep us busy most of the day getting it stacked in the barn."

"Hot work," Eva observed with sympathy.

"The kind that makes a man appreciate a cold drink and shade at the end of the day," Cade agreed. "What about you? More work on the website?"

Eva's face lit up with excitement. "Actually, Mom's coming over in a little bit, and we're going to go through aunt Connie's old recipes and test out a few."

"Sounds like you'll have a good day. You can bring Noah over to the ranch later if you want. Your dad and I can keep an eye on him.

"I may just do that."

Chapter 43

Friday, July 3rd...

"Cade!" Noah's excited voice rang out across the morning air before Cade had even shut his truck door. The boy bounded down the porch steps wearing khaki pants, a button-down shirt, and his best boots.

"Mornin' little man," Cade said, noting how Eva sat on the porch in a soft green sundress and sandals, her hair styled and makeup applied. She looked beautiful.

"We've been waiting for you," Noah announced as he reached Cade's side, practically vibrating with energy despite the early hour. "Mom says we're going to Billings today, but I don't want to go."

Eva stood and walked to the porch railing. "Mornin' Cade."

"Mornin'. What's happening in Billings?" Cade asked, climbing the porch steps to join them.

"Business paperwork," Eva explained, smoothing down her dress with nervous hands. "I need to file the final documents for the bed and breakfast license and get all the tax information sorted out. While

I'm in the city, I figured I'd get ahead on school clothes shopping for Noah. Might as well take care of it all in one trip."

"But I don't want new clothes. I don't want to go to the city," Noah interjected with the dramatic despair of an eight-year-old facing a fate worse than death. "I want to stay here and do ranch stuff. Please, Mom?"

"Noah, I can't leave you here all day."

"Why not?" Noah asked with perfect eight-year-old logic. " I'll be really good. I promise."

"He'd be fine with me," Cade said.

"Are you sure? I know you and Dad have work to do, and I don't want Noah to be a distraction."

"He's never a distraction," Cade said honestly. "Right, partner?"

"I'm the bestest helper!" Noah declared.

Eva sighed in defeat. "All right. You can stay. But," she held up a warning finger as Noah started to cheer, "you have to promise to listen to Grandpa and Cade and do exactly what they tell you. No arguing, no wandering off, and no getting into things you shouldn't."

"I promise!" Noah said, already starting to hop down the porch steps in his eagerness to begin his day. "Can we go now?"

"Hold on there, cowboy," Eva called after him. "You need to change out of those good clothes first. Put on your work jeans and boots."

Noah skidded to a halt and raced back toward the front door. "I'll be super fast... don't leave!" he called over his shoulder as he disappeared into the house.

Eva turned to Cade with an expression of mixed gratitude and concern. "Thank you for offering to watch him. I know he can be a handful when he gets excited."

"No thanks needed," Cade said, settling against the porch railing. "Besides, your dad and I can use an extra pair of hands today."

"He's growing up so fast. Sometimes I look at him and wonder where my little boy went."

"He's still there," Cade assured her. "Just getting more capable every day. You should be proud of the great job you're doing with him."

"I hope so. Some days I feel like I'm making it up as I go along."

Eva reached into her purse and withdrew a folded piece of paper, extending it toward him with a smile.

"Before I forget," she said. "And before Noah comes thundering back down those stairs."

Cade accepted the note, noting how Eva stepped closer as he unfolded it.

"Also," Eva continued, her voice taking on a casual tone that didn't quite hide her hopefulness, "I was wondering if you'd like to go to the Fourth of July parade tomorrow evening? Then the fireworks in the town square afterward."

"Sure. Sounds like the perfect way to spend the holiday."

"Good," Eva said, her smile brightening. "The parade starts at seven."

"It's a date," Cade replied.

"Come by in the morning around 9 for breakfast? I want to make one of Aunt Connie's breakfast casserole recipes, and you can be my taste tester."

"I can do that."

The sound of footsteps thundering down the stairs interrupted the moment as Noah reappeared, now dressed in work jeans, boots, and a t-shirt that had seen better days.

"Ready!" he announced breathlessly. "Can we go now?"

"Go ahead," Eva said with a laugh, pressing a quick kiss to Noah's forehead before he could dodge away. "Remember… listen to Grandpa and Cade and be good."

"I will!" Noah called, heading toward Cade's truck with the boundless energy of a boy who'd just been granted his greatest wish.

Eva turned back to Cade, who was still holding her unopened note. "Read that later. If and when you have a quiet moment."

"I will," Cade promised, tucking the paper safely into his shirt pocket.

As Eva gathered her purse and headed toward her SUV, Cade called after her. "Drive safely. And don't worry about Noah—I'll take good care of him."

"I know you will."

Cade watched her drive away, then looked at Noah, who stood beside his truck.

"Ready to go have some fun?"

"Ready!" Noah declared, climbing into the passenger seat with the excitement of someone embarking on the greatest adventure of his life.

Cade pulled Eva's note from his pocket before they left:

"The Lord is my rock, my fortress and my deliverer; my God is my rock, in whom I take refuge, my shield and the horn of my salvation, my stronghold." Psalm 18:2

Chapter 44

aturday, July 4th...

"He gives strength to the weary and increases the power of the weak."
Isaiah 40:29

Eva noticed Cade staring up at the darkening sky, his expression distant despite the excited chatter around them. Families filled the town square with quilts and lawn chairs, children ran between the adults with sparklers, and the anticipation of fireworks charged the evening air. But Cade seemed a million miles away.

"You okay?" Eva nudged his shoulder gently.

Cade blinked and turned to her with a small smile. "Just thinking about that Bible verse you shared at breakfast this morning."

Noah sat on the quilt nearby, his cowboy hat slightly askew. "When do the fireworks start?"

"Soon, sweetheart," Ruby said from her lawn chair, reaching over to straighten his hat.

Chuck stretched his legs out on the quilt and adjusted his position. "Best fireworks show in three counties. Been coming to this since I was younger than you."

"Really, Grandpa?"

"Yep. My mama and daddy brought me every year, just like I brought your mama when she was little, and now she's bringing you."

Eva smiled, then glanced back at Cade. He'd been unusually quiet. The parade had been wonderful—Noah waving at every float, Cade's hand warm in hers as they walked along Main Street, the whole town coming together in celebration.

"What about the verse?" she asked quietly.

"Strength to the weary," Cade said, his voice barely audible over the crowd noise. "I've just been thinking about life in general... how my life had been empty."

A whistle screamed overhead, followed by a boom that made Noah gasp with delight. The first firework exploded in brilliant gold above them, painting their faces in warm light.

"Here we go!" Noah shouted, pointing up as red, white, and blue cascades filled the sky.

Eva watched her son's wonder-filled face for a moment, then looked at Cade. The colored light played across his features as he watched the display, but she caught him glancing at her more than once.

"Then what?" she prompted during a brief lull between explosions.

"Then you came home," Cade said simply. "And everything changed."

Another series of fireworks lit up the night—silver willows that dripped like tears, followed by chrysanthemums that bloomed and faded in rainbow colors. The crowd oohed and ahhed with each new display.

Noah leaned back against Eva's legs, his excitement finally calming into contentment. "This is awesome."

After fifteen full minutes of impressive fireworks, the grand finale began: rapid-fire explosions that turned night into day and left the crowd cheering and applauding. Noah scrambled to his feet to get a better view, Ruby and Chuck pointing out different effects, the whole square alive with celebration.

As the last echo faded and people began gathering their things, Eva started folding the quilt while Noah helped Chuck with the lawn chairs.

"Ready to go?" Ruby asked, shouldering her purse.

Cade surprised Eva by taking the quilt from her and reaching for her hand.

They walked slowly behind her parents and Noah, the crowd streaming around them toward the parking areas. Main Street buzzed with conversations about the show, children begging for just five more minutes, and teenagers making plans to meet up later.

Halfway to their cars, Cade stopped and turned to face her. His hand was warm around hers, his expression serious in the glow of the streetlights.

"Eva," he said quietly, leaning close enough that only she could hear. "I love you. More than I did all those years ago. I've always loved you."

Eva's heart started beating so hard she was sure everyone in town could hear it.

Without hesitation, she rose on her tiptoes and pressed a soft kiss to his cheek. "I love you too," she whispered. "So very much."

When she pulled back, Cade's smile was brighter than any firework she'd witnessed earlier.

Chapter 45

*S*unday, July 5th...

"See! The winter is past; the rains are over and gone. Flowers appear on the earth; the season of singing has come, the cooing of doves is heard in our land." Song of Songs 2:11-12

Chapter 46

Monday, July 6th...

"Do not gloat over me, my enemy! Though I have fallen, I will rise. Though I sit in darkness, the Lord will be my light." Micah 7:8

Chapter 47

"I don't know, Luke," Cade said into his phone, running his free hand through his hair. "It's complicated."

Eva stepped into the barn carrying a container of fresh-baked cookies, planning to surprise Cade with an afternoon snack. But his voice stopped her just inside the doorway. His back was toward her, and something in his tone made her hesitate.

"Yeah, I know the money sounds great," Cade continued, pacing a few steps before stopping abruptly. "Twice what I'm making now, and you're right about the housing market in Colorado. I could actually afford something."

Eva's heart sank. Luke—Cade's cousin in Colorado. She remembered him from their high school days.

Cade shook his head. "But that's not..." He paused, listening. "No, I get it. It sounds like a good opportunity. Great opportunity. I just..."

He trailed off, and Eva could see the tension in his shoulders, the way he shifted his weight from foot to foot like a man caught between two impossible choices.

"Look, can I think about it?" Cade asked. "I know you need an answer soon, but there are things here I need to consider. People I need to... yeah... Yeah, I understand... Give me two days, and I'll call you back with an answer."

He ended the call and stood motionless, staring down at his phone. Eva cleared her throat.

Cade spun around. "Eva... How much of that did you hear?"

"Enough to figure out you've been offered a job elsewhere."

Cade slipped his phone in his pocket and leaned against the nearest stall door. "My cousin Luke runs a big operation outside Denver. His foreman's retiring, and he wants me to take over. It's..." He gestured helplessly. "It's twice what your dad pays me."

Eva nodded slowly, her face carefully neutral. She walked over and extended the container of cookies toward him. "Sounds like you have a lot of thinking to do."

Cade accepted the cookies but didn't open the container. "Eva—"

She was already turning to leave.

"Eva, wait." His voice stopped her at the barn entrance. When she turned to face him, her expression was unreadable.

"I need your advice on this," he said.

Eva studied his face for a long moment. "I have none to give," she said quietly. "This is something you need to work through on your own."

She turned and walked away, leaving Cade standing alone in the barn with a container of cookies.

Chapter 48

*T*uesday, July 7th...

Cade pulled up to the bed and breakfast at his usual time, but the porch was empty.

He sat in his truck for a moment, engine idling, staring at the vacant porch. Had he ruined everything with one phone call? Was she done with him?

He spotted a white piece of paper wedged between the screen door and the door frame. His heart lurched. She wasn't giving up on him. She was giving him space.

Cade climbed out of the truck, his boots heavy on the gravel drive. The morning air felt different without Eva's warm greeting, silence where her laughter should be.

He climbed the porch steps and reached for the folded paper and opened it with hands that weren't quite steady.

"In their hearts humans plan their course, but the Lord established their steps." Proverbs 16:9.

I trust the Lord with your future, even if it looks different than you expected.

Cade sank into Eva's usual chair, the note trembling in his hands. She wasn't trying to influence his decision. She wasn't angry or hurt or manipulative. She was trusting God with his choice, even if it meant losing him.

Chapter 49

Two days now of arriving to emptiness where warmth used to be. Cade cut the engine and stared at the vacant wicker chairs, the small table bare of coffee cups.

Cade's chest tightened.

He walked to the porch, each step echoing in the morning quiet. The paper crinkled softly as he unfolded it. Eva's familiar handwriting steadied him even as the words made his throat tight:

"You will keep in perfect peace those whose minds are steadfast, because they trust in you." – Isaiah 26:3

Perfect peace.

Cade folded the note and slipped it into his pocket.

He looked toward the ranch, then back at the house where his heart lived.

Chapter 50

Cade sat on his front porch, forearms resting on his knees, staring out at the pasture where Storm grazed in the late afternoon sunlight, wrestling with a choice he'd already made. Two days of Eva's quiet faith reaching him through carefully chosen verses tucked against her door. Two days of knowing exactly what he wanted but feeling like a man standing at the edge of a cliff, terrified to jump.

The sound of hoofbeats interrupted his brooding. Chuck rode across the pasture on his gelding, Ranger, moving with the confidence of a man who knew his place in the world.

Chuck dismounted near the cabin, his movements deliberate and unhurried. He dropped Ranger's reins to let the horse graze, then climbed the porch steps without a word and settled into the second rocking chair. The wood creaked under his weight as he removed his hat and set it on his knee, his weathered hands folding across his stomach.

For several minutes, they sat in silence, both men gazing out at the rolling pastures and the ranch beyond.

"Been a good day for moving cattle," Chuck said eventually. "Cool enough to work hard, warm enough to enjoy it. Always appreciate a good day like this."

Cade nodded. "Storm worked like a champion today. That bull gave us trouble, but Storm anticipated every move."

"Good horses are like good friends," Chuck observed, his eyes crinkling slightly. "They know what you need before you ask for it."

Another silence settled between them, broken only by the gentle sound of the horse tearing grass and the distant lowing of cattle.

"You've been awfully quiet the past couple of days," Chuck said finally, his tone casual but his eyes perceptive as they studied Cade's profile. "Walking around like a man with something heavy on his mind. Care to talk about it?"

Cade leaned back in his chair, the wood creaking softly. His hands gripped the armrests as he gathered courage. "My cousin Luke called Monday. Offered me a job in Colorado. Foreman position on his operation outside Denver."

Chuck's expression didn't change, but Cade caught the slight tightening around his eyes. "That so? Is it a good outfit? What kind of offer did he make you?"

"Twice what you pay me. Housing allowance, full benefits, profit sharing. I could buy a place of my own eventually and have something to show for my work." He paused, then added quietly, "He runs a good outfit."

Chuck was quiet for several minutes, his fingers drumming softly against his stomach. When he spoke, his voice was neutral. "Sounds like a good opportunity. What decision are you leaning toward?"

"Already made it," Cade said. "Hours after Luke called, I knew I didn't want the job. Called him back that evening and declined the offer."

Chuck turned to study Cade's face more directly, his weathered features showing surprise. "Just like that?"

"Just like that," Cade replied, meeting Chuck's gaze. "I thought on it for a few hours… I mean, who wouldn't?"

"Then what's got you sitting out here looking like the weight of the world's on your shoulders? You're regretting turning down the offer now… aren't you?"

Cade was quiet for a long moment, gathering courage for words that felt too big and too important to say out loud. The late afternoon breeze rustled through the cottonwood trees, and somewhere in the distance, a coyote called to its pack. When he finally spoke, his voice was rough with emotion he'd been holding back for days.

"No… the problem is, Chuck, I've never stopped loving your daughter. Not for a single day in twelve years. I realize that now. And now that she's back… now that I know what it feels like to have her in my life again… I don't want to lose her." He paused, swallowing hard. "I want to marry her. Not someday, not after we've dated for a year or two. Now."

Chuck's eyebrows rose slightly. "Well, then what are you gonna do about it?"

Cade looked at him with a mixture of surprise and frustration. "What do you mean, what am I going to do about it? Seems a bit too fast, doesn't it? People will think I've lost my mind."

He chuckled, the sound warm and knowing. "Son, you two have been in love since you were seventeen years old. You and I both know that."

"But what if—"

"What if what? What if she thinks you're rushing things? What if people talk? Which by the way… let 'em talk. What if you're not good enough for her?" He shook his head. "Cade, I've watched that girl of mine for thirty years. I've seen her in love exactly twice in her life. Once with you and once with David. She doesn't give her heart lightly, and when she does, it's completely."

Cade gripped the armrests of his chair tighter, his knuckles white. "I made such a mistake, Chuck. The biggest mistake of my life."

"What mistake is that?"

"Letting her go when we were eighteen. I didn't want to break up with her. God knows I didn't want that. I wanted to marry her right out of high school. I wanted to build a life with her on my family's ranch and wanted to wake up next to her every morning for the rest of my life."

Chuck leaned forward in his chair, giving Cade his full attention. "Then why did you let her go?"

"Because I thought I was doing the right thing. I thought I was being noble, giving her the freedom to experience life and go to college without feeling tied down to some small-town cowboy. I didn't want to hold her back from her dreams, didn't want her to wake up ten years later and resent me for keeping her from the life she could have had."

"So you sacrificed your happiness for hers."

Cade nodded. "Turns out I just made myself miserable for twelve years. If I could go back, if I could change things..." He shook his head. "I would fight for her. I would tell her I can't live without her and ask her to marry me."

Chuck was quiet for a long moment, processing Cade's confession. "You know what I think?" he said finally.

"What?"

"I think you did exactly what a good man would do. You put her happiness before your own, even when it broke your heart. That's not a mistake, son. That's love." Chuck paused, his voice growing gentler. "But you're not eighteen anymore. And neither is she. You're both adults who've lived enough life to know what you want and what you don't want."

"She was married before," Cade said quietly. "She knows what a good marriage looks like. What if I can't live up to David's memory? What if I'm not enough for her and Noah?"

Chuck's expression grew stern. "Now you listen here, Cade Mayer. I watched that girl grieve her husband, and I watched her raise that boy alone for eight years. She did it with grace and strength and more courage than most people possess. But you know what I've seen in her face these past weeks that I haven't seen since she was eighteen years old?"

"What?"

"Joy. Pure, uncomplicated joy. The kind that comes from being exactly where you're supposed to be with exactly the person you're supposed to be with. Eva has been half-alive for eight years, going through the motions of living but not really living. You came back into her life, and she started blooming again like a flower that finally got enough sunlight."

Cade felt his throat tighten with emotion. "You think?"

"I know so. And you want to know something else? Noah needs you just as much as she does. That boy has never known what it's like to have a father, and he found one in you. You think Eva doesn't see that? You think she doesn't know what a gift you are to both of them?"

"I love that boy like he's my own."

"He is your own," Chuck said firmly. "In every way that matters. Love makes a family, not blood."

They sat in silence for several minutes, both men lost in their own thoughts as the stars began to appear in the darkening sky. Finally, Chuck spoke again, his voice quiet but certain.

"You want some advice from an old man who's been married to the same woman for thirty-two years?"

Cade nodded.

"Don't wait. Life's too short and too uncertain to waste time being cautious when you know what you want. Eva's not a teenage girl anymore—she's a woman who's faced loss and hardship and come out stronger. She doesn't need time to figure out her feelings. She knows exactly what she wants, and if these past weeks are any indication, what she wants is you."

"What if I'm not good enough for them?"

Chuck reached over and clapped a firm hand on Cade's shoulder. "Son, you are good enough. The only person who doesn't see that is you."

Chuck smiled, his eyes twinkling with something that looked suspiciously like mischief. "First thing you're gonna do is ask my daughter to marry you. And you're gonna do it right—none of this casual, maybe-someday nonsense. You're gonna get down on one knee and tell her you want to spend the rest of your life loving her and Noah and any other children God might bless you with."

"And if she says yes?"

"When she says yes," Chuck corrected, "you're gonna marry her as soon as she'll let you. Life's too precious to waste, and you two have wasted enough time already."

Cade felt a smile tugging at the corners of his mouth for the first time in days. "I have your blessing?"

Chuck stood up, settling his hat back on his head. "Son, I think my daughter's been waiting for you to ask her to marry you since she was eighteen years old. You have my blessings... and by the way... it's about darn time."

Chapter 51

*T*hursday, July 9th...

"And hope does not put us to shame, because God's love has been poured out into our hearts through the Holy Spirit, who has been given to us." Romans 5:5

Chapter 52

F riday, July 10th…

"He who was seated on the throne said, I am making everything new!"
Revelation 21:5

Chapter 53

Friday, July 10th...

Eva stared at her computer screen, trying to focus on the email from a potential guest inquiring about weekend rates. The words blurred together as her mind wandered for the hundredth time that morning. Four days since Cade had learned about the job offer. Four days of silence between them, of her giving him space to make his choice while her heart twisted with worry.

She forced herself to type a response about room availability and local attractions. At least work kept her hands busy, even if it couldn't quiet her thoughts.

"Vroom! Crash!" Noah's sound effects drifted up from the rug where he was orchestrating an elaborate car accident with his toy collection. "Mom, the red car needs to go to the hospital. Can you be the ambulance?"

"Just give me one minute, sweetheart," Eva said, attaching photos of the guest rooms to her email.

She clicked send.

"Eva? Noah?" Ruby's voice called from the front entrance.

"In here, Mom," Eva called back, rising from her desk chair as her mother appeared in the office doorway.

Ruby wore a cheerful yellow blouse and carried her purse over her shoulder, her car keys jingling in her hand. "There you are. I was hoping I could steal my grandson for the day."

Noah looked up from his cars, his face lighting up. "Where are we going? Somewhere fun?"

"Very fun," Ruby said with a grin. "We need to run errands in town, maybe stop by the library, and I thought we could get ice cream at that new place on Main Street."

"Can I, Mom?" Noah was already scrambling to his feet, his car collection forgotten.

Eva nodded. "Of course. Just be good for Grandma and don't wander off."

"I'm always good," Noah protested, earning a laugh from Ruby.

"What about you, honey?" Ruby asked Eva. "What are your plans for the day?"

Eva glanced at her computer, then back at her mother. "Finishing up some emails. And now that I'll have a few hours to myself, I think I'll start painting my bedroom. I've been putting it off long enough."

"That sounds like a good project," Ruby said. "Are you all right? You seem a bit..."

"I'm fine," Eva said quickly. "Just a lot of stuff going on right now."

Ruby studied her for a moment longer, then nodded. "Well, if you need anything, call me. We'll probably be gone most of the day."

Noah hugged Eva goodbye, his small arms fierce around her waist. "Love you, Mom."

"Love you too, buddy," Eva said, kissing the top of his head.

She followed them outside, standing on the front porch as Noah chattered excitedly about their plans while Ruby helped him into the car.

Eva waved as they drove away, Noah's face pressed against the window as he waved back. She remained on the porch, watching until the car disappeared around the bend and the dust settled back onto the gravel road.

The silence that followed felt enormous.

She sank into one of the wicker chairs, her hands folded in her lap, and let herself think the thoughts she'd been avoiding all morning. What if Cade had decided to take the job? What if he was planning to leave and didn't know how to tell her?

The questions circled in her mind like vultures, each one picking at her confidence. She'd been so sure, so certain that they were finally on the same path. But maybe she'd been naive. Maybe love wasn't enough when a man had been broken the way Cade had been.

Eva closed her eyes and tried to pray, but the words felt tangled in her throat. Instead, she sat in the morning stillness and fought the urge to walk to the ranch and find Cade and demand answers.

Should she seek him out this evening when he finished work? Should she wait for him to come to her? The uncertainty was eating her alive, but she'd promised herself she wouldn't pressure him. This choice had to be his alone.

Even if waiting for his decision was slowly breaking her heart.

Chapter 54

Eva dipped her brush in the taupe paint, carefully working it into the corner where the wall met the ceiling. Her bedroom was finally taking shape. Paint dotted her old jeans and the faded t-shirt she'd chosen for the messy work, and her hair had long since escaped its messy bun to frame her face in paint-streaked tendrils.

She stepped back to admire her progress, envisioning how beautiful the room would be when finished. Aunt Connie's antique furniture would look perfect against these walls, and the morning light streaming through the turret windows would create the perfect place for her to start her day. A place of rest, just like she'd always—

"MOM!"

Noah's voice from downstairs startled her so badly she nearly dropped her brush. A drop of paint splattered onto her shirt, adding to the collection she'd already accumulated.

"Coming!" she called back, setting her brush on the paint tray and wiping her hands on an old towel. She hurried toward the stairs.

As she descended from the third floor to the second, she heard her mother's voice, unusually excited: "Now be still... hold it just like this..."

"I got this grandma..."

Eva paused, frowning. What was her mom up to? And why did Noah sound so... different? There was something in his voice she couldn't quite place. Excitement? Nervousness?

She continued down the flight of stairs toward the main floor, wondering what kind of surprise awaited her. Probably something Noah had bought in town that he wanted to show her.

Eva stopped short, her hand gripping the banister as she took in the scene before her. Noah stood in the center of the foyer, his face bright with the biggest grin she'd ever seen, his hands clasped behind his back. Beside him stood Cade, looking nervous, his hat in his hands and his green eyes fixed on her with an intensity that made her heart skip.

Her parents stood to one side, her father's arm wrapped protectively around her mom's shoulders. Everyone was looking at Eva with expressions of barely contained excitement and anticipation.

"What's this?" Eva said when she reached the bottom step of the staircase.

Without a word, Noah and Cade dropped to one knee simultaneously. Noah brought his hands forward, revealing a burgundy velvet box that looked enormous in his small fingers. He fumbled with it, his excitement making his hands shake.

Eva tilted her head, her heart beginning to race.

"Hold on," Noah muttered, still struggling with the box. "This thing is... there!" The box finally opened with a soft click, revealing a ring that caught the afternoon light streaming through the stained glass window and threw rainbows across the foyer walls.

Noah looked up at her with eight-year-old directness, his voice clear and hopeful: "Will you marry Cade, Mom? I want him to be my dad. He let me help pick this out!"

Eva's hands flew to her face, covering her mouth as a gasp escaped. She looked between her son and Cade, then at her parents. Her mother was crying, happy tears streaming down her cheeks, while her father's eyes were suspiciously bright.

"Mom?" Noah prompted when she didn't respond immediately. "You look funny."

A laugh bubbled up from Eva's chest, somewhere between joy and shock. She stepped down from the stair, her legs unsteady as she moved toward them. Cade was still on one knee, his eyes never leaving her face, waiting.

"I..." Eva's voice caught in her throat. "I don't know what to say."

"Say yes," Noah said helpfully. "Cade told me he loves you, and I told him I love him too."

Eva's heart melted at her son's simple logic. She looked at Cade, who was carefully taking the ring from the box with trembling hands. The diamond was perfect—not too big, not too small, classic and elegant in a simple setting.

"Eva," Cade said, his voice rough with emotion. "I've been trying to find the right words for days, but Noah here told me I was overthinking it." He glanced at the boy beside him, who nodded encouragingly. "He said I should just tell you how I feel."

"That's what I said," Noah confirmed proudly.

Eva laughed through tears she didn't realize had started falling. "You did, did you?"

"Uh-huh. And I told him, You've been sad, and I don't like it when you're sad."

Cade's eyes grew tender as he looked at Noah, then back at her.

"Eva," Cade began again, holding the ring between them. "Twelve years ago, I made the biggest mistake of my life. I let you go because I thought I was doing the right thing, giving you the freedom to chase your dreams. I should have asked you to marry me then and figured out a way to make it work."

"I won't make that mistake again." He took a shaky breath. "I love you. I've never stopped loving you, not for a single day. And I love Noah like he's my own son, because in every way that matters, he is. You two are my family, my home, my everything."

"Mom," Noah whispered loudly, "I think you're supposed to say something now."

Eva laughed, wiping tears from her cheeks.

She looked at Cade, this strong, gentle man who'd found his way back to her through heartbreak and healing, through faith and forgiveness. "I love you too," she said.

"Is that a yes, Mom?" Noah asked. "My knee is starting to hurt, and Cade said we had to stay like this until you answered."

Eva laughed, the sound bright and joyful in the afternoon light. "That's definitely a yes."

Cade's face broke into a smile that rivaled the sun as he slipped the ring onto her finger. It fit perfectly, catching the light from the stained glass window and throwing tiny rainbows across their joined hands.

"I'm not letting you go ever again," he said, his voice fierce with promise.

Noah whooped with delight, jumping to his feet. "I'm gonna have a dad!" He threw his arms around both of them, squeezing tight. "Best day ever!"

Eva looked at Cade, seeing her own joy reflected in his eyes. "The very best day," she agreed.

From across the foyer, Ruby's voice broke through their moment: "Well, are you going to kiss her or not, Cade Mayer? That's how these things are supposed to end!"

Noah giggled and stepped back. "Yeah, you're supposed to kiss Mom!"

Cade stood, his hands framing Eva's face gently. "May I?"

"I thought you'd never ask," Eva whispered.

When their lips met, it was everything a kiss should be—tender, sweet, and full of promise. It was the seal on a love that had weathered separation and heartbreak, that had grown stronger and deeper with time and trial.

When they broke apart, Noah was grinning up at them. "So what now? How do you get married? When?"

Eva and Cade looked at each other and burst into laughter, the sound echoing through the foyer of the house where their new life together was just beginning.

"Soon," Cade said, ruffling Noah's hair. "Very soon."

"Good," Noah said with satisfaction. "Because I'm not very good at waitin'."

Eva's heart overflowed as she looked at her son, then the man who would be her husband, and then her parents, who were beaming with joy.

She was home. They were home. And they were never letting go again.

EPILOGUE

Saturday, August 1st...

Eva smoothed her hands over the pale ivory satin and lace dress she'd chosen as she stood with her father on the front porch of the Lost Creek Bed & Breakfast. The late afternoon sun cast everything in golden light, and the mountains beyond seemed to approve of the day's celebration.

"You look beautiful, sweetheart," Chuck said, adjusting his tie nervously.

Eva smiled, feeling radiant in ways that had nothing to do with the dress or the flowers Ruby had woven into her hair. "I feel beautiful, Dad."

Chuck offered his arm. "You ready?"

"I've been ready," Eva said, slipping her hand through the crook of his elbow.

They walked around the side of the house, Eva's heart racing with anticipation. As they rounded the corner, the backyard came into view, and Eva's breath caught at the sight before her.

Ruby and the other ladies from church had transformed the space into something magical. White chairs arranged in neat rows faced a simple wooden arch that her dad had built and her mom had decorated with wildflowers and flowing ribbons. The arch stood beneath the old oak tree where Eva had played as a child, its branches creating a natural canopy overhead. Mason jars filled with more wildflowers hung from the tree's lower branches, and a white runner stretched down the grass aisle.

Every seat was filled with neighbors, church friends, ranch hands, and business owners from town. Pastor Sam stood beneath the arch in his best suit, his Bible open in his hands and a smile bright enough to rival the sun.

But Eva's attention was captured completely by the two figures waiting for her at the altar.

Cade stood tall and handsome in a dark suit, his usually unruly hair neatly combed, his green eyes fixed on her with an intensity that made her knees weak. The boy she'd fallen in love with at seventeen was gone, replaced by a man who knew exactly what he wanted and wasn't afraid to reach for it.

Beside him stood Noah, vibrating with excitement in his first real suit. Her son—their son—had insisted on standing with Cade instead of walking down the aisle, declaring that he belonged "with his dad." The sight of them together, both waiting for her, made Eva's heart overflow with joy.

The gentle strains of "Canon in D" began to play from the small quartet of musicians Ruby had arranged, and Eva felt her father's arm tighten beneath her hand.

"Here we go," Chuck murmured, and they began their walk down the aisle.

Eva was aware of the smiles and happy tears around her, of Lily Hawthorne wiping her eyes with a handkerchief, and of the ranch hands who'd cleaned up especially for the occasion. But her focus remained on Cade, whose face broke into that smile she'd fallen in love with all those years ago.

When they reached the altar, Chuck lifted Eva's hand to his lips for a gentle kiss, then placed it carefully in Cade's waiting palm.

"Take care of my girl," Chuck said, his voice thick with emotion.

"Always," Cade replied, his eyes never leaving Eva's face.

Chuck stepped back to take his place beside Ruby, who was dabbing at her eyes with a tissue. Pastor Sam cleared his throat and began the ceremony.

"Dearly beloved, we are gathered here today to witness the union of Eva and Cade, two souls who have found their way back to each other through faith and the unfailing love of God..."

Eva heard the words, but her attention was focused on Cade. This was the man who'd helped her son learn to ride, who'd fixed her plumbing disasters, and who'd returned to faith through her patient encouragement. This was the man who'd chosen love over fear and who'd chosen her.

"Do you, Cade, take Eva to be your wife, to love and cherish, in sickness and in health, for richer or poorer, forsaking all others, as long as you both shall live?"

"I do," Cade said, his voice strong and certain. "I absolutely do."

"And do you, Eva, take Cade to be your husband, to love and cherish, in sickness and in health, for richer or poorer, forsaking all others, as long as you both shall live?"

"I do," Eva whispered, then repeated it louder, her voice ringing with joy.

Pastor Sam smiled. "The rings?"

Noah stepped forward importantly, producing the wedding bands from his pocket with the careful precision of someone who'd been practicing this moment for weeks. He handed Cade's ring to Eva and Eva's ring to Cade, then whispered loudly, "Don't drop them!"

The congregation chuckled, and Eva felt her heart swell with love.

They exchanged rings with promises of forever, their voices strong and certain as they spoke the words that would bind them as husband and wife. When Pastor Sam pronounced them married, the cheer that went up from the crowd was led by Noah's excited whoop.

"You may kiss your bride," Pastor Sam said with a grin.

Cade stepped closer, and instead of the gentle kiss of new love, he dipped her dramatically, sweeping her backward as his lips found hers in a kiss that spoke of passion and promise and a lifetime of tomorrows.

The crowd erupted in applause and cheers, but Eva heard only the sound of her own heartbeat and Noah's delighted laughter as he danced around them, shouting, "They're married! They're really married!"

When Cade lifted her upright, Eva's face was flushed with happiness. "Hello, husband," she said softly.

"Hello, wife," he replied, his voice thick with emotion. "Best day ever?"

Eva looked around at the faces of everyone she loved—her parents beaming with pride, the community that had welcomed her home, the ranch hands who'd become family, and, most importantly, her son, who was still dancing with joy at having gained not just a dad but a complete family.

"Best day ever," she said, meaning it with every fiber of her being.

27 Days of Encouragments

D^{ay 1}

"Trust in the Lord with all your heart and lean not on your own understanding; in all your ways submit to him, and he will make your paths straight." - Proverbs 3:5-6

Day 2

"Forget the former things; do not dwell on the past. See, I am doing a new thing..."– Isaiah 43:18–19

Day 3

"The Lord is close to the brokenhearted and saves those who are crushed in spirit." – Psalm 34:18

Day 4

"A cheerful heart is good medicine, but a crushed spirit dries up the bones." – Proverbs 17:22

Day 5

"Do not fear, for I am with you... I will strengthen you and help you." – Isaiah 41:10

Day 6

"For I know the plans I have for you... plans to give you hope and a future." – Jeremiah 29:11

Day 7

"Be strong and courageous... for the Lord your God is with you wherever you go." – Joshua 1:9

Day 8

"He heals the brokenhearted and binds up their wounds". – Psalm 147:3

Day 9

"There is therefore now no condemnation for those who are in Christ Jesus." – Romans 8:1

Day 10

"The old has gone, the new is here." – 2 Corinthians 5:17

Day 11

"The Lord your God... will take great delight in you... He will rejoice over you with singing." Zephaniah 3:17.

Day 12

"Come to me, all you who are weary and burdened, and I will give you rest."Matthew 11:28.

Day 13

"The Lord is my strength and my shield; my heart trusts in him, and he helps me." Psalm 28:7.

Day 14

"Being confident of this, that he who began a good work in you will carry it on to completion until the day of Christ Jesus." Philippians 1:6.

Day 15

"Therefore, my dear brothers and sisters, stand firm. Let nothing move you. Always give yourselves fully to the work of the Lord, because you know that your labor in the Lord is not in vain." 1 Corinthians 15:58

Day 16

"Your word is a lamp for my feet, a light on my path." Psalm 119:105.

Day 17

"Let us not become weary in doing good, for at the proper time we will reap a harvest if we do not give up." Galatians 6:9.

Day 18

"He will cover you with his feathers, and under his wings you will find refuge; his faithfulness will be your shield and rampart." Psalm 91:4

Day 19

"Because of the Lord's great love we are not consumed, for his compassions never fail. They are new every morning; great is your faithfulness." Lamentations 3:22–23

Day 20

"The Lord is my rock, my fortress and my deliverer; my God is my rock, in whom I take refuge, my shield and the horn of my salvation, my stronghold." Psalm 18:2

Day 21

"He gives strength to the weary and increases the power of the weak." Isaiah 40:29

Day 22

"See! The winter is past; the rains are over and gone. Flowers appear on the earth; the season of singing has come, the cooing of doves is heard in our land." Song of Songs 2:11-12

Day 23

"Do not gloat over me, my enemy! Though I have fallen, I will rise. Though I sit in darkness, the Lord will be my light." Micah 7:8

Day 24

"In their hearts humans plan their course, but the Lord established their steps." Proverbs 16:9.

Day 25

"You will keep in perfect peace those whose minds are steadfast, because they trust in you." – Isaiah 26:3

Day 26

"And hope does not put us to shame, because God's love has been poured out into our hearts through the Holy Spirit, who has been given to us." Romans 5:5

Day 27

"He who was seated on the throne said, I am making everything new!" Revelation 21:5

Leave A Review

If you enjoyed this book, please consider leaving an honest review
on Amazon

Visit Our Website:

www.tarabaisden.com

Visit Our Amazon Author Page HERE

Find Us On Social Media:

Facebook

Facebook Author Page

Instagram

About The Author

Tara Baisden is a Contemporary Christian Inspirational Romance author who proudly calls the beautiful state of West Virginia her home. Nestled on a sprawling mountainous property, she is surrounded by the peace and serenity of nature. Her days are happily spent in the quiet of country life, writing heartwarming stories of love, faith, and second chances. Tara also enjoys quilting, working in her garden, tending to her beloved pets, and soaking in the beauty of her surroundings.

With deep roots in West Virginia, family is everything to Tara. One of her favorite pastimes is gathering on the front porch with loved ones, sharing stories, laughter, and enjoying the simple, meaningful moments that life offers. When she's not crafting her novels, Tara can often be found exploring the rich history of her home state, visiting local historical sites, and, of course, stopping by every bookstore she passes! Her passion for reading and discovery always fuels her next adventure.

Tara is the author of the Laurel Ridges series of novels, as well as the Riverbend Valley series of novels, of which have been beloved by fans of inspirational romance. Her novels reflect her love for faith, family, and the timeless beauty of the world we live in.

Known for her sweet and clean romances, she creates characters that feel like family and settings that make readers want to visit again and again.

You can find out more about Tara and her latest releases at www.tarabaisden.com or follow her on social media for updates and behind-the-scenes glimpses of her writing process. Stay connected—you won't want to miss the heartfelt stories of love and family she has in store!

Also by Tara Baisden